BAD LIKE ME

ROYAL BASTARDS MC

CHELLE C. CRAZE
ELI ABBOT

Bad Like Me © 2020 Chelle C. Craze & Eli Abbott

All rights reserved. Except as permitted under the U.S. Copyright Act of 1976, no part of this publication may be reproduced, distributed, or transmitted in any form or by any means, or stored in a database or retrieval system, without prior written permission of the author.

The scanning, uploading, and distribution of this book via the Internet or via other means without the permission of the publisher is illegal and punishable by law.

Please purchase only authorized electronic editions and do not participate in or encourage electronic piracy of copyrighted materials. Your support of the author's rights is appreciated.

Bad Like Me is a work of fiction. Names, characters, businesses, places, events, and incidents are either the products of the author's imagination or used in a fictitious manner. Any resemblance to actual persons, living or dead, actual events, or locales is entirely coincidental.

The author acknowledges the trademarked status and trademark owners of various products referenced in this work of fiction, which have been used without permission. The publication/ use of these trademarks is not authorized, associated with, or sponsored by the trademark owner.

Otherwise, hold on and enjoy the ride, you crazed lunatics!

Editing & Proofreading by: Maria Vickers
Cover by: Simply Defined Art

Created with Vellum

I can't dedicate this book to who I wish, because it has cuss words and he wouldn't appreciate that...so this book is for you, (insert your name). You're fabulous, beautiful, and all kinds of other flattering words. Seriously, you are, though.

SYNOPSIS

The majority of people thought all bikers, especially one-percenters like us, handled things the same. Those people would be irrevocably wrong. Our now rival MC, The Dogs of Chaos, was proof. Their club's greed outweighed the amount of honor they had for our deal. We were quick to remind them what a colossal mistake they made. I was the Vice President of the Cleveland, Ohio Chapter of the Royal Bastards MC. My cut was sacred, and I wore our colors with pride.

I thought of my past daily, but that didn't mean I still loved her. The remnants of guilt I felt in my gut every day didn't prove that I should have followed her. They were reminders of my life, a part of the history of how I became who I am: a stubborn SOB with a foul mouth and a heap of felonies. Stealing guns, arson, breaking and entering, these were all petty things to me. My only weakness was admitting my true feelings for her, and I refused to...until I was forced.

When Ray abruptly walked into my life again, or rather, I barged into hers, I quickly vowed this time would be different. The thing was, a person couldn't make promises without considering the rest of their life, particularly someone with as many enemies as I had. I stupidly got caught up in the moment and forgot who I was and what that meant for her. I never meant for any of it to happen; I didn't want this for her.

The Dogs would retaliate for our transgressions; this much I was certain of. Having knowledge didn't make a difference in the end, because what they took from me could never be replaced. I was Logan "Crow" Williams, and just like a crow, I would hunt them down and reap my revenge in blood.

ROYAL BASTARDS MC SERIES

Erin Trejo: Blood Lust
Chelle C Craze & Eli Abbott: Bad Like Me
K Webster: Koyn
Esther E. Schmidt: Petros
Elizabeth Knox: Bet On Me
Glenna Maynard: Lady & the Biker
Madison Faye: Hard Bastard
CM Genovese: Frozen Rain
J. Lynn Lombard: Blayze's Inferno
Crimson Syn: Inked In Vengeance
B.B. Blaque: Rotten Apple
Addison Jane: Her Ransom
Izzy Sweet * Sean Moriarty: Broken Wings
Nikki Landis: Ridin' For Hell
KL Ramsey: Savage Heat
M.Merin: Axel
Sapphire Knight: Bastard
Bink Cummings: Switch Burn
Winter Travers: Playboy
Linny Lawless: The Heavy Crown

Jax Hart: Desert King
Elle Boon: Royally Broken
Kristine Allen: Voodoo
Ker Dukey: Animal
KE Osborn: Defining Darkness
Shannon Youngblood: Silver & Lace

Royal Bastards MC Facebook Group - https://www.facebook.com/groups/royalbastardsmc/
Website- https://www.royalbastardsmc.com/

ROYAL BASTARDS CODE

PROTECT: The club and your brothers come before anything else, and must be protected at all costs. **CLUB** is **FAMILY.**

RESPECT: Earn it & Give it. Respect club law. Respect the patch. Respect your brothers. Disrespect a member and there will be hell to pay.

HONOR: Being patched in is an honor, not a right. Your colors are sacred, not to be left alone, and **NEVER** let them touch the ground.

OL' LADIES: Never disrespect a member's or brother's Ol'Lady. **PERIOD.**

CHURCH is **MANDATORY.**

LOYALTY: Takes precedence over all, including well-being.

HONESTY: Never **LIE, CHEAT,** or **STEAL** from another member or the club.

TERRITORY: You are to respect your brother's property and follow their Chapter's club rules.

TRUST: Years to earn it...seconds to lose it.

NEVER RIDE OFF: Brothers do not abandon their family.

Can't you see you're like me
Guilty
A sinner from the pain
Close your eyes
And be poisoned
Poisoned by the blame
Walking the path of darkness
Crawling, Shaking chains
Fed by lies of beauty
Destruction fueling the flame
Just one look could kill you
But you'll chance it chasing fame
I'll ruin you she whispered before ice formed in her veins
Staring at me, she cried out
While her eyes staked their claim
Can't you see you're like me
Guilty
A sinner from the pain
Close your eyes
And be poisoned
Poisoned by the blame
Defenseless screaming shadows slither in your brain
She'll fade away to gravity
Drowned by the day
Can't you see you're like me
Guilty
A sinner from the pain
Close your eyes
And be poisoned
Poisoned by the blame
Powerless to her tonic
Her lips blew out the shame

I breathed in the corruption
A guilty shaking cave
One day you'll be like me
Guilty
A sinner of the pain
But tonight I'll be your poison
As I watch you fade away

1

RAY

Logan "Crow" Williams stole my heart prior to either of us ever having the knowledge of the very real and boundless significance of the cliché saying. It wasn't one that could easily be taken in stride. It was his before I was aware someone could own the majority of someone else simply by being who they were. It didn't matter, though. Sometimes, you didn't have to understand things for them to have meaning. I was his. It always made sense until life and time intervened with responsibilities, pressuring us with expectations of becoming an adult.

He was mine long before he was known as "Crow". To me, he was simply Logan. My Logan. Most of what happened might be chalked up to ignorance...or maybe it was puppy love. Really, I had absolutely no idea what it was exactly that drew the two of us together. Was it fate that brought us together or was it real love that we shared? Was it the genuine thing most people coveted only to believe that when they didn't have it, it only happened in books? Convenience? Maybe it was just being in the right place at the right time? The only thing I was certain about, we were something special to one another back in the day. However, where and what we were to each other was more than a mystery. We quickly found out belonging to someone else could be extraordinarily messy and unbelievably complicated; and yet, we were too young to ever acknowledge the strength of the words we were saying. Regardless of how things ended, it wouldn't have stopped us. We were both too stubborn—and I most certainly was now—to listen to someone else when it came to things I was passionate about.

Every so often, you had to amble into the past, if only to remind yourself of how to move forward again. That was what I told myself I was doing when I thought of Logan, relearning the steps that brought me to where I was today. Learning how to walk again came with ease some days, and others, well, it was more of a crawl through my memories, eventually making it back to reality.

It'd been seven years since we parted, and I moved to Kentucky to chase my dream job. Over two thousand five hundred and fifty-five days had passed since we'd agreed to go our separate ways, so why would I still care for him? I didn't. Okay, I did, but I wasn't sure where those emotions found meaning in the stupid constricting muscle inside my chest and the feelings buried deep within my mind. I obviously loved him and always would, but I wasn't in love with him. We'd both decided it was for the best that I move out here to put my electrical engineering degree to good use because I was in so much debt for the schooling that I had to figure out how to pay back the student loans.

We didn't share the same values anyway, and in the beginning, that didn't hold much importance at all. Yet as time passed, it became clearer than anything else. I wanted him to come to college with me in Kentucky. He wanted to remain in Ohio to eventually take over his dad's shop. I begged him to let me stay, but we both knew I would go in the end. Of course, we tried the long-distance thing, but once he joined the Royal Bastards MC and I made the dean's list, it became harder to travel the distance and easier to make excuses. I'd never know if we made the right choice by letting each other go, but did one ever know the realness of their choices until it was much too late? Anyone who said they did was a damn liar, but for me, I still wasn't sure of the correct answer.

From time to time, I thought of him and kept tabs on him, or rather, my best friend, Wren, kept me up to date on things since she still lived in our hometown of Cleveland, Ohio. Even when I told myself I didn't want to hear about him, on the days I knew I didn't have the strength to walk, those moments when it would be more of a sluggish crawl kind of day, he seemed to grace the conversations between Wren and me. She knew me well, was fully aware that I wanted to know how he was even if I didn't allow myself to bring him up. Somehow, it made it easier if I wasn't the one asking, but relentless curiosity brewed within me, and Wren understood that.

Somedays, like today, I told myself I wouldn't check on him, which simply meant not answering the phone when I saw Wren's name and the goofy picture she made me take appear on the screen of my cell phone each time she called.

Wren: Don't ignore me. I know you're awake and probably just sitting around working on some animatronic cock pump.

I glanced at the phone as it lit up and vibrated against my desk but didn't respond. I wouldn't touch my phone while working on hospital equipment because even though everything was allegedly disinfected before it came to our department, it occasionally still had blood on it and who knows what else we couldn't see. This was all true, but it didn't mean I wasn't thankful I couldn't respond to her right now.

> **Wren: Paging Dr. Jo Harding, put Dorothy down for a minute. I need to talk to you.**

I laughed and shook my head as I tightened the thin metallic bracket down onto the plastic door and popped it into place.

"Ray, you have a call on line one," Matt, our lead technician, announced after he answered the office phone and swirled around in his comfy chair to face my desk.

"One sec," I answered, propping the base of the infusion pump I was in the middle of repairing onto the handle of a Phillips screwdriver and huffed. Flipping the lever down, I ground my teeth. I'd been trying to do a performance check on this fucking pump for the past hour, and the phone was ringing nonstop with tasks I had to do.

"Is it the third floor again?" I smacked my lips together, certain they were calling to complain about one of their thermometers being on the fritz again. I already explained twice this morning that if they cleaned the lens with alcohol, the fucking things would work properly, but the first time apparently hadn't sunk in, and it was clear now the second hadn't either. I hoped it was them because if Wren was calling here, she had finally given up on any and all boundaries.

"No. It's...ummm..." He held a finger up and pressed the button to remove the caller from hold. "Who did you say this was?" He adjusted his glasses on the bridge of his nose and eventually pushed them onto the top of his head amongst his thick silver hair. "I see. I'll let her know." His tone immediately changed from his original businesslike voice to a serious one.

My heart rapidly pounded behind my ribs with fear, and I swallowed hard in anticipation. It was rare to see Matt cross the line of professionalism on the phone, so when he did, the whole crew felt it. Walsh and I exchanged a knowing look as his blue eyes widened while I shrugged my shoulders. "No fucking clue," I said in a voice barely above a whisper, and both of us stared at Matt for answers.

"It's your mom," Matt told me in a weak voice and slowly blinked his eyes.

Momentarily, my eyelids closed and reopened with new tears on their brims. Mom wouldn't be calling me at work unless something was wrong. My parents were more than proud of me and where I had taken my career. Because of this, they refused to call during work hours even though I told them that if it was important, it didn't matter.

"Hello?" I nervously forced from my dry throat as I placed the black receiver to my cheek and untangled the cord. "Fucking mess," I murmured, flipping the phone outward and pulling at the curled wire.

"Excuse me?" Mom all but shouted into my ear as soon as I put it against my head, and my hand flew up to cover my mouth.

"Sorry, Mom. What's wrong?" I probed, getting right to the point. Some families pussy-footed around things, but that wasn't us. It had never been. We'd been through too much to worry about the pleasantries every other family had the luxury of observing. At least, it wasn't how I handled things, my parents, on the other hand, were a completely different story.

"It's Dad."

"What about him?"

"The doctor said the prognosis is a good one. Fuck, I'm sorry I called. I shouldn't have, but I didn't know what to do." She sobbed when the last few words left her lips. "I'm sorry, Rachel. You know how I feel about doctors and their 'everyone is going to be okay' bullshit. It's just...it's back," she whispered. "He wasn't going to call you. Hell, he didn't want me to, but he doesn't have the energy to get out of bed most days now. He doesn't know I'm on the phone with you. I just...had to tell you. You needed to know."

"It'll all be okay, Mom. I promise." I cringed as the lie slithered up my windpipe, and it constricted as I forced the deceptive words to find volume and meaning. "I'll be there as soon as I can."

Every set of eyes in the shop was now on me and impatiently awaiting the next words to leave my lips. I was the type of person who didn't get incredibly personal with anyone, but over the past few years, working alongside these guys, I'd opened up to them. They all knew my dad wasn't in the best of health and that I would drop everything if I had to for him.

"No, Ray. I don't want you to do that. We don't want you to give up your career for us," Mom sighed on the other end of the call and was, no doubt, pacing the small space in the bathroom of our three-bedroom home. It was where she made all of her calls she didn't want Dad to overhear.

"Mom, it's cancer. It took Grandma and Granddad. I won't sit idly by eight hours away just to get another phone call telling me that my dad is dead. I won't do it. I'll be there before you know it," I promised, sucking back the ball of regret growing by the minute in the center of my throat. I should have moved back the first time he got cancer, but the doctors promised they had caught it early enough to get rid of it, and they thought they had. Evidently, they had not.

"Okay, Ray. Do what you have to do but don't flush your dream job down the drain just to rush home and take care of us."

"I won't. It'll be okay. Jerry will understand; he's a down to earth type of boss," I lied again, knowing damn well as soon as I informed him I was leaving, I wouldn't have a job waiting for me when I returned. At this point, I didn't care. I could always find another job, but no one in this world could ever replace my dad.

"Are you sure?"

"One-hundred percent. Everything will be fine on my end, Mom. There's just no need for you to worry about me right now." I reassured her, breathing another white lie of comfort into her ear. On a general note, I hated lying. Right now wasn't any different, but what else was I going to say? Mom, I'm leaving my job and have no fucking clue what I'll do for income. The answer was no. I wouldn't tell my mom I was dropping everything to rush home for them. It wasn't what any good child did once they grew into adulthood, much to the contrary. Parents spent a good deal of their lives giving everything they had to ensure their children had everything they needed—any parent worth a shit anyway. It was the morally right thing to try and take care of your parents when they couldn't quite care of themselves anymore. It was the law of nature, so to speak. All of this made sense to me, but to someone else, it might be a foreign concept. Other people didn't matter in this situation. For me, nothing else held importance, only my parents and their well-being. After all the madness settled, I would be left to collect the shambles of my so-called-life, and then I would figure out my next move. But for now, it didn't matter. I had to get to them. Any second I wasn't with them was wasted time.

"Just as long as you're sure," she weakly said, sniffing back the new wave of emotions that hit her.

"I am." Once again, I deceived my mom because it was a necessity, fully aware I was fucking over everything I'd work toward in the past seven years, and yet, not caring about it.

I wished it had been Wren on the phone wanting to talk about something trivial, but I now realized, she more than likely didn't want to mindlessly chitchat and wanted to find out how I was handling things. Wren had probably talked to Mom first, so I texted her.

Me: Dad is sick.

Tears of regret streaked down my face as I stared at those three bold words on the screen in my hand, and my bottom lip quivered as I tried to keep it together in the shop. A soft sob left my mouth, and I covered it behind my cupped palm, pushing the shop door open and running into our breakroom. Walsh was right behind me, no doubt searching for an explanation. None of my coworkers had ever seen me cry —not too many people had, actually. I avoided it at all costs since I wasn't a dainty crier. When I cried, I sobbed. It was as if once the tears finally broke free, the amount that fell made up for all the times I refused to shed a tear.

"My dad's cancer is back," I told him in an almost inaudible tone, trying to compose myself. Maybe if I talked about it, I could calm down. Perhaps it could make sense as to why such a good man had cancer not once, but twice. I guess it was possible his body had the disease all along and we didn't know about it.

"I'm sorry," he said in a similar voice and took a seat at our table, pulling a seat out for me to sit beside him.

The phone vibrated in my palm, and I glanced at it.

Wren: I know :(I tried to catch you before you left for work, but I had to keep Bologna for Logan, and lucky me, he found a rat. Ham just wanted to play with it...Never mind. I'll tell you later. How are you doing?

A laugh bubbled through my body and then another. The first came at the thought of my best friend having a rat in her apartment—she was terrified of them. The second because those two were the only people in this world who would name their animals after lunchmeat. Bologna was Logan's horse of a dog, and Ham was Wren's black cat.

"It's funny?" Walsh looked at me over the black square frames of his glasses and kept his attention on me.

"Yes. Well, no. This is." I dropped into the blue plastic chair beside him, setting my phone in front of him.

"Does Wren...uh, you know?" He pinched his thumb and pointer finger together and hit an imaginary joint.

Another laugh shook my body and quickly left as I swiped away the remaining tears off of my cheeks. "No."

"No? Her ham is playing with a rat that bologna found," he pointed out and shrugged, forcing a fake smile. "I mean, I'm not one to judge, I smoke, but hell, that's a little farfetched even for me."

"Ham is her cat, and Bologna is her brother's dog," I explained, typing out a reply to Wren and began planning what would have to be done before I could leave for Ohio.

Me: No fucking clue, but I'll be there as soon as I can. You have a rat?

Wren: Apparently. Huge fucker, too. I'll be here when you do

2
CROW

"Diablo, I gotta be somewhere, so can we please move this shit along?" I loudly muttered over the rattling of the chain as he cut it in two, and I ran my rough fingertips over my beard. He glared at me, catching the lock in his palm as it released from the chain.

"Fucking man up, Crow. We have to get this shit done. They crossed the line this time. These motherfuckers owe us these guns, even if they don't think they do. They're ours. They should have kept up their end of the deal, and we wouldn't be taking the whole lot. Oh well, c'est la vie." Diablo smiled, pulling a rag from his pocket and rubbing his prints off the silver metal before tossing it into the grass.

"I know. The fuckers screwed us over. These are our guns, no question. But if your slow ass doesn't hurry up, this is about to be a solo mission," I snapped out of frustration, questioning Ghoul's decision for sending me on such an important trip with a careless shit like Diablo. He was my brother, and I trusted him with my life as I did with any of our other brothers, but Diablo wasn't my first choice for an accomplice. Hell, he wasn't even my second in line for the job. I would have taken any other brother from the Royal Bastards MC. He was too impulsive and unpredictable for my liking. I heard Jameson was headed back to New Orleans, I'd give my left nut to have him by my side or the right for Koyn from our Tulsa Chapter to be here. Fuck, Sleeper and Sledge would have been perfect for this job, but they were on the road somewhere between here and West Virginia moving Roane's Old Lady's shit.

Diablo was notorious for being loud as fuck and couldn't diffuse a situation to save his life, hence his road name. He hadn't gotten it for being the best in situations such as this. More often than not, he went into things with guns blazing and always left a fucking mess behind him. He was the type to shoot first and ask questions later. Maybe that was why Ghoul chose him as my second for this; Diablo was a sharpshooter, spook veteran from the army. It could have been we were the perfect combination of reason and chaos, but in my opinion, the two of us gave the very definition of disaster to the dictionary.

Our now rival MC, The Dogs of Chaos, had taken the guns we were supposed to split fifty/fifty and ignorantly stored them all at the same location we'd agreed to do so in the first place. The problem was, it was their warehouse, not ours.

The plan had been that after Sledge, Flashman, and Circuit headed the truck off at the West Virginia/Ohio line, The Dogs were to grab the goods and meet up with us later. The problem was, they never showed. After the whole debacle went down, it came to light that their state boss decided to keep the guns for their brothers and cut our club out of the deal. That didn't go over well with any of us Bastards, so here I was with the loudest mother fucker on the planet doing a B&E to take what was owed to us, trying to keep his ass in check so I could go to a funeral I wouldn't be very welcomed at.

"Remember what Ghoul said, grab what we can and then get the fuck out of dodge," I quietly reminded Diablo as he slowly stepped into the warehouse behind me. Flipping a switch to his right, he waited for something to happen. Clearly, he hadn't been paying too much attention when we met with The Dogs since they told us the switch didn't work; therefore, I didn't stand around like a dumbass or look up expecting lights to brighten.

"Yeah, Crow. I got this shit. Quit trying to be my mom and pull the truck up." He laughed, plucking his keys from his pocket and adjusting his fresh cut. It hadn't been too long ago that he was patched into the Bastards, so he took every chance given to bring attention to his leather. It might have impressed the club whores and even the prospects, but it did nothing for me. I had almost three years on him in the club, and my cut was so worn, it didn't even smell like leather anymore. It had more of a lingering scent of exhaust and booze to it. It was seasoned, unlike him or the leather strapped over his torso.

"I'll get the truck but remember your place, Diablo," I barked, instantly pissed that he had the balls to call me his mom, even if I knew damn well his point was more than valid. I was over hesitant and filled with anxiety. None of it was related to what we were doing, though. We would get the guns and not run into a problem, and if we did, we would handle it. I didn't give a shit how many motherfuckers had to die, the job was finished when I left.

Hell, the reason I was on edge had nothing to do with our club. If I was being honest with myself, it had everything to do with my past I was willingly throwing myself into the damn middle of after working so hard to get away from it.

Ray was back in town. Of course, she was. Her dad had died, and it was his funeral I was in a rush to get to. I didn't know if I was nervous about seeing her or her dad's lifeless body, but I refused to face that dilemma right now. I had to stay on point for our mission. When a dumbass wasn't focused, that was when mother fuckers wound up dead. I planned to wreak havoc on this world for at least a couple more years, so I cleared my head of everything apart from the here and now. I would deal with the rest of it when I had to, but until then, it was an out of sight out of mind type of thing. It had to be.

"I know. I know. You're the VP, and I'm just a peon, but we're brothers all the same. I'm in this shit with you, brother." He clapped me on the back and smiled. "Fuck the world, right?"

"Yep. Fuck. The. World." I tried to stop the smirk as it crept onto my lips, but I couldn't. He was right. Fuck the rest. I was here with my brother and the remainder of the world and its occurrences didn't matter at the moment. We had a job to do, and we would get it done. It was as cut and dry as that, regardless if I was nervous as fuck to see her. The fact I had counted the days that had passed since we'd last spoken wasn't important right now. What I had to focus on was keeping my brother and me alive and bringing back the goods that rightfully belonged to the Bastards. The rest of the world would just have to fall to the wayside because first and foremost, I was a Royal Bastard, and then I was Logan Williams. Even though my legal name was rarely spoken anymore, it didn't matter, there was still a past, and a long story that came along with it—one I didn't revisit often because it wasn't exactly who I was anymore. There was a thing about a person's past, it didn't matter what amazing or shitty things you did to create a future, there would always be someone from your past to tug you back into it. Some people easily forgot yesterday, and some still lived in the days most had forgotten.

"You get the cage." I chuckled, dropping his key ring into his open hand and pulled a crowbar out of the exposed toolbox beside me. "You're right. I am the vice, and if anyone is taking lead on this one, it's me."

"There he is," Diablo admired, turning to leave me and get the vehicle.

"What do we do with this place?" Diablo asked, loading the last crate into the back and closing the doors behind it.

"Board up the windows and torch that mother fucker!" I shouted. "No one fucks with the Royal Bastards. This will make them remember that!" I grabbed a gas can, flipping the lid open, and doused everything surrounding me.

"Damn straight, brother. Damn straight," he repeated, pulling a matchbook from his pocket, and a deep sadistic laugh left his body. "Nobody fucks with the Royal Bastards."

3

RAY

I hated this day, but I think that I hated myself even more. Despite how fast I dropped my life and moved back to Ohio, it wasn't enough. Mom let me know dad was bad, but she hadn't been exactly forthcoming with all of the information. She told me it was cancer, but not that the doctors had basically said it was inoperable. The fucking disease had spread its poison throughout his entire body and had taken over most of it. Maybe he could have tried radiation, but we learned that would have been meaningless for him at that point. It was only an option for someone it the earlier stages of the illness, not at the end, which was where he was.

Dad's body was tired and riddled with something modern medicine had yet to find a miracle cure for. The thing about cancer was, once its necrosis began, there was typically no stopping it. For him, there wasn't an option to take a pill for seven to ten days to heal him—a luxury too many of us have when we go to see the doctor and tell them that we feel like we were dying. My dad actually was dying. He was too far gone to be saved.

I'd been here for a little over a week, and he didn't recognize me during the majority of the days spent with him. He had moments of clarity, though. Those were the times I would cherish and cling to on the hard days. The days when I wanted to give up but couldn't let myself crumble. I hoped it was how I would remember him instead of delirious and fragile.

We talked as if our world wasn't being destroyed with every second that passed. He told me he was so proud of me and loved me more than anything. He asked about my job and how I liked living in Kentucky. I didn't have a chipper answer at first but wished to see him smile, not bring him down with me, so I lied. The first lie led to a second, and before I was aware of it, I had created an entire fictitious life and didn't stop until we were both satisfied. I told him my life was great and couldn't wait for Mom and him to visit during the summer, knowing it was doubtful he would see the sunrise again and definitely would not be here during his favorite time of the year, spring. When he mentioned my love life, I said I was happy that my career kept me too busy to date and rarely thought about the fact that I lived alone, although it was something I thought of every night before my eyes closed. Of course, he knew me well enough to realize the answers I gave him held little to no truth, but he didn't punk me out on it. Therefore, I kept painting the beautifulness of a perfect life that I lived for him. He wouldn't get to see how my life turned out, and neither of us could begin to guess where it was headed, but we both liked the story I told.

When he faded out of reality, I whispered lies of my wedding and how he had to catch me from falling as he walked me down the aisle. I told him he secretly hated the guy I was marrying, but only because he didn't think the guy was good enough for his little girl. Dad tried to laugh at that one, but it came out as a faint noise accompanied by a bright smile.

"Course he isn't." Dad grinned, and his eyelids blinked slowly while he attempted to fight the drugs coursing through his veins. "Nobody will ever be good enough for my Ray." He barely forced the words out of his lips before soft snores took their place.

"Tell me more. What about Momma and me?" He quietly encouraged without reopening his eyes.

"We all drive Hummers."

"No!" His eyes flickered open momentarily with excitement and were fast to close again. "Ferraris."

"Okay, Dad." I laughed and shook my head, another small giggle piping through my lips. "We all drive Ferraris, and I make so much money, we live in a fucking castle with all the works. A private jet and butlers."

His eyebrows rose high on his forehead when I cussed, but I hadn't expected less. Actually, I was selfishly hoping it would pump a little fire into his body and remind him how to fight. I needed him to fight, but it was a losing battle. I wasn't an idiot. You couldn't ask someone to switch positions in the middle of a war after they'd been shot while standing guard on the frontline of duty. That was basically what I was doing, asking the impossible from my dad. I wanted to witness him being the only person to recover without any treatment...that I knew of anyway. The rest of society and their anomalies didn't matter to me, they weren't my dad. In the end, the heart-shattering devastation was that it didn't matter how much we both wished for none of this to be real, it was. He was slipping closer to death with every word we spoke, and it didn't matter if either of us wanted it. He was dying, and I would keep living without him.

It was funny, people who weren't apt to lie frequently did

in times like this. I was no different. I couldn't bear the thought of telling him I regretted moving away a little more each time I entered his room. I wouldn't breathe the truth that every constriction of my heart hurt more than the last because I'd spent so much time away from them. These talks were limited, and I never knew from one minute to the next if I was talking to the real dad or if it was the drugs speaking for him.

A nurse explained the morphine would help him rest, and he wouldn't be in as much pain. When his breathing was fast, I noticed they gave it to him more than when it wasn't. Seeing all of the tubes and wires connected to the man who taught me to ride a bike and throw a right hook was never something I thought I would live to see. It was definitely a sight I hoped I wouldn't. On the last day, we both felt it coming. He waited until Mom left the room and opened his palm for me to put my hand in it.

"Rachel Charlene. My Ray of sunshine," he paused, and his chest rapidly heaved as he caught his breath, exhausted from the short sentences he spoke. "Promise me you'll take care of her. I know it's a lot to ask, but I don't think I can keep up my end of the bargain anymore," he panted in a very weak voice, and his light blue eyes filled with tears of shame. He was never one to quit anything, much less admit defeat, but here he was doing exactly that. I wanted to hate him for giving up, but it would be selfish to do. He'd fought for so long. Honestly, I had no clue how long he'd struggled to keep his life on this earth, battling the death rapidly pulling him into the afterlife. I was ashamed that I didn't know how long he had been sick. I should have asked more than I had, but I didn't, and it was something I would always regret.

"I promise, Dad, I'll take care of Mom." I sniffled as tears circled the whites of my eyes and trickled down my cheeks, one pooling around my nose ring as I wiped it away.

"If you didn't have all that tackle in your beautiful face, that wouldn't happen." He attempted to laugh but ended up coughing instead.

"It gives me character." I meekly smiled, repeating the words he'd repeated to me countless times when people had made fun of my piercings. That was the thing about my dad, he always had the right words to say at the exact moment they needed to be said. I'd promised to take care of Mom, but I would always be playing second fiddle to him. If I had to be a second chair to someone in life, I was honored it was him.

TODAY WASN'T GOING to be easy. How did one prepare to bury their dad? The person who taught them to be strong and fought off the bad begging to bleed into one's mind? You didn't. Plain and simple. No amount of time or planning could ever make me ready to face this day. Even if I had a thousand years to get ready for this, I still wouldn't be prepared for it.

I'd been in a daze of denial right up until the moment we picked out his casket and made the arrangements, but putting on an all-black outfit and experiencing the quietness of my childhood home, made it even more real. There wasn't any music flowing through the open air of our home as there would have been if he were still here with us. The faint and comforting whisper of *Don't You Cry Baby* wasn't lingering in the background of my every movement in this house as it had as long as I could remember any time Dad thought I was feeling down. The irony of the lyrics wasn't lost on me, but I ignored it. I didn't want to accept that he was gone. I couldn't. My parents were the one constant in my life that had always been there for me. Even on the shittiest of days, Mom and Dad were in my corner, and often Mom and I fought too much to have long conversations. Dad was always the one to have heart-to-hearts with me, but those wouldn't happen anymore. The song that was a better fit for today was *Drown In My Own Tears*. While I hadn't let myself truly embrace the feelings of loss that pulsated through my whole body, I felt the meaning of that song more now than ever before. I was drowning myself in torture and grief, and now, there wasn't a person alive with the strength to pull me from the tragedy of my own mind. The rain of sadness filled my insides, and I didn't know what I would do when it spilled over and left me gasping for air.

I stood as still as possible, hoping any song in my Dad's voice would somehow find its way into the air on its own, but the only thing pounding in the stagnant almost unbreathable atmosphere was the silence of death. We all made promises to loved ones of what we would do if something ever happened to them. I wasn't any different. I'd vowed to dad on one of his good days that I would blast Ray Charles through the walls of our house as a reminder that we would all be together again one day. I hadn't only broken that promise, I made one to myself. Not only would I not play the songs by him, but I would avoid anything that reminded me of this place. It made me a shit daughter, but I planned on begging Mom to move to Kentucky with me as soon as everything settled down. I would still take care of her, but it wouldn't be here where all the good memories of my once happy family transitioned into ones of failure.

I couldn't stay here. Everything I saw reminded me of Dad and how I let him down. Maybe if I hadn't left, maybe then, he'd still be alive. Fuck. I really had no conception of reality at this point or what I would have done to prevent what happened to him, but anything was better than what I did...or rather, what I hadn't done. Absolutely nothing. Not a damn thing. I didn't do a thing to stop his death, not that I really could have had I been here, but I could have visited more. I hadn't been back home since two Christmas's ago. These were the things that would haunt me for each day to pass. The what-ifs and what could have been's could very well be the reason I joined Dad in death. Could a person really worry themselves to death or was it merely a figure of speech? I had no clue, but the way my sides were heaving in and out with distress and the unrelenting pain forcing its way through my body made it pretty evident. It was a very real possibility. Guilt had far more power than anyone ever gave it credit for unless they happened to be experiencing it like me.

"We have to go, Ray," Mom called up the stairs, her voice carrying into my room.

I shivered as she spoke my nickname, feeling the overwhelming guilt that landed on me with it. Dad and his love for Ray Charles' music. No matter how much I wanted to forget, I would always be a constant reminder of the ways I abandoned my dad when he needed me the most. He once said he named me after the only other thing he loved, other than Mom that was, music. Mom wouldn't let him name a girl simply Ray, so he picked the name Rachel Charlene since it was essentially Ray Charles' name, give or take a couple of different letters here and there.

I didn't answer her as I should, I merely powered down my cell and shoved it into my clutch as I slowly inched my arm through the strap to drag out the moment. Each step I took drew me closer to the second we dropped my dad six feet under the earth, and I wasn't ready for any of it. This was a portion of life no one should ever have to experience, and yet, we all did. We all encountered the death of loved ones, never truly knowing how to handle it. Death was one of the subjects no one really knew how to approach. We were all as clueless as the next when it came to grieving. No one possessed the capability of delivering the correct words to make another long any less for yesterday because those words didn't exist. At the end of the day, the person was still gone, and despite how much any of us tried, it wouldn't change a damn thing.

Many familiar faces paused in front of Dad's casket and then paid their respects to us as we sat in the front pew of the church. The majority of people said they went to wakes and graveside services to pay their respects, but it wasn't to the dead as most thought, it was to those left behind. That was exactly how I felt. Dad left me behind, and now, I didn't know what to do with my life. Clearly, I could have just asked for some time off work instead of quitting, but whatever amount of time work gave me would never be enough. I had to be here with Mom because I wasn't here for Dad. I vowed to myself that I wouldn't leave her to wither away without him. Here I was, in Cleveland, Ohio, jobless and falling apart from every cell in my body.

I sat almost motionless, transfixed on the sunlight bleeding through the stained-glass window as if in a trance. Both the light and window were beautiful, but somehow lost their luster as they fell into the darkness of sorrow. The only time I looked at the faces that approached thereafter was when I was spoken to directly, which wasn't often. Most of the people were here for Mom and had long forgotten me. Either that or they didn't have any words of comfort for me, so they didn't even try. Of course, Wren was seated beside me and held my right hand in her left. I didn't ask if Logan was going to be here because I was afraid of the answer she would give me.

I wasn't sure if I would be happy or devastated to cross paths with Logan again. Something deep inside my body ached for him to be here, maybe he could make this nightmare disappear. I wasn't stupid, I knew it wasn't true, but it didn't stop the longing from happening. Even if he did show, I wouldn't know him any more than he would me. No single person was to blame for that. We were both at fault. Maybe we didn't fight hard enough for us, or maybe we pushed the whole "us" too far. I hated how selfish I was at this moment. My thoughts should have been filled with memories of Dad, but here I sat a measly eight feet from his lifeless body thinking of my past relationship.

4

CROW

Even though I rode my bike hard and fast, I didn't make it to the services on time. I blame Diablo's slow ass. People were filing out of the church and climbing into their vehicles when I arrived, and I wasn't a complete dick, I didn't want to bust into the service at the conclusion. I respected Rich too much to do that. When my mom and dad were conveniently absent for the important things of a teenager's life, Rich, Ray's dad, was always there for Wren and me. Hell, he had been there for me while Ray was gone. He was someone I could always talk to when I didn't have anyone else outside of the clubhouse to confide in. He may have been her father by blood, but he was important to me, too—even if Ray was oblivious to that fact.

The truth was, I had no idea how much or little she knew about me or my relationship with her parents. When Rich wasn't there for me, Mary was. Mary wasn't only Mom's best friend, she took care of us when Mom wasn't able. When Mom couldn't afford my tux for prom, Mary paid for it with no questions asked. The only two people who were let in on that secret were involved in the conspiracy: Mary and me. Mom didn't know where I got the money for it, and she didn't ask, so I didn't tell her. She would have been embarrassed to know that Mary paid for it and would've tried to give her the money back, money we didn't have to give. If it hadn't been Ray's dream to go to prom together, I would have said fuck it to the whole thing; prom really wasn't my scene, anyway. It didn't matter, though, it was what Ray wanted, so it was what I had to do because I loved her.

I wanted to be here for the wake because I didn't do well with funerals, not since Mom's. I had only been to one since she passed and didn't plan to attend another anytime soon. It wasn't anything personal to Ray, more like every time I saw a body being dropped into a grave, their face morphed into Mom's. I couldn't do it. I wouldn't watch my mother be buried every time someone else died, so I stayed away from the event entirely. The one and only graveside service I attended after Mom was in remembrance of our Uncle Stephen, and it was then I learned I couldn't attend another funeral again. It wasn't that I didn't want to be present for the people I cared about, I did. It was just I wasn't physically able to do it. Losing Mom was one of the hardest things I'd dealt with in my life, and I'd committed countless crimes without losing too much sleep. My transgressions didn't compare to funerals.

My tires ground against the gravel of the parking lot as I turned them to the left as hard as I could and headed toward the clubhouse before anyone spotted me. There was no use hanging around here where I would be faced with uncomfortable questions I refused to answer.

Wren stopped at the bottom of the church steps, her

eyes locking with mine as my Harley rolled to a halt at the stop sign, and I dropped my boots against the pavement to support the weight of my bike and me. She hatefully glared at me and then glanced at her cell phone, no doubt checking the time, and shook her head. My shoulders simply rose and fell in a nonchalant shrug, and I took off, the tire treads gaining asphalt as quickly as I could make them. The fact that she clocked my time would work to my benefit, even if I hadn't planned for her to do so. It would give me a timeline and an alibi, not that I thought The Dogs had the balls to involve the law, but I could only speculate what they would do. They were one-percenters like the Royal Bastards. Without a shadow of a doubt, I knew none of us would be phoning the pigs because as a rule, the colder we were on their radar the better.

AS SOON AS I was through the clubhouse door, Ghoul passed me a handle of whiskey. He was pleased with the guns, which was good because when he was unhappy, it was hard to be around him. He nodded his head in appreciation and clicked his tongue against the roof of his mouth before calling his shot, "Eightball, corner pocket." He pointed the tip of his stick toward the far-left end of the table, aimed, and sunk the black ball exactly where he said he would.

"Good one, Boss," I congratulated him and walked toward the bar. Ghoul could run the table on about anyone who walked into our clubhouse. Depending on how cocky his opponent was, set Ghoul's level of seriousness, and he'd been known to put money on the games on occasion. It was usually his way of reminding people to be humble and would shut them the fuck up about how good they thought they were. Ghoul was a hell of a President and liked people to remember their place in the world. He and I shared the belief that we're all people, only some of us have different titles, and some are shittier than others. It made us damn good leaders for the club and was a good reminder when either of us needed a swift kick in the ass to bring us back down to earth.

An exasperated huff left Circuit's lips when I dropped my ass onto my usual stool right of the bar door. He was on bar duty, and he hated every minute of it, but somebody had to do it. There were many reasons a brother would be behind the bar serving everyone else. We all took turns, but it could also be a form of punishment when someone fucked up. The latter was the reason Circuit was pouring the drinks tonight, and he knew it. Hell, we all did.

"Circuit, you'll be off duty next week, right?" I cleared my throat after taking a few big swallows of whiskey and wiped my mouth on the back of my forearm, trying to remind him he wasn't on a life sentence behind the bar.

"That's the word…as long as I keep the customers happy." He half-heartedly smirked, grabbing the ashtrays and emptying them one at a time into the trashcan underneath the bar's surface.

"Just keep your shit together, and Ghoul will let you off. You're just the patsy for losing the guns."

"What about Ghoul getting off? This is a conversation I should be a part of." Ghoul's bass voice boomed through the clubhouse, and he plopped down onto the stool beside me. "Heh. I like getting off, so this topic is of particular interest to me. Ain't that right, Red?" he called over his shoulder to a normal club whore as she bent over the pool table behind us to take her shot, standing as straight as an arrow when he called her name.

"Sure do, Ghoul." She giggled, wiggling her ass and popped it out further than necessary as she pressed her tits against the green felt of the table to take her shot.

Fucking club skanks. I would be a liar if I said I had never indulged in a few of them, but I made damn sure I always wore a rubber. Who knew what any of them had—probably more than I wanted to think about, honestly. Who in their right mind would willingly be treated like shit and have no purpose other than being used as a fuck doll? I wouldn't that was for certain. Maybe that was the reason I hated them so much—I just didn't understand them. They obviously didn't have any self-respect because if they did, they wouldn't be here doing what they did. There was no lingering question in my mind that all of these bitches had daddy issues or something equally as severe, none of those things crossed my mind anytime any of my brothers or I needed to get off. It made me a hypocritical asshole, but I didn't seem to feel much remorse when I was balls deep. Why would I? It wasn't like anyone forced them to be here; they came through the door of their own free will, and when they were fucked, they were fucked well. Unless, of course, they were unlucky enough to end up in bed with Sac. If they did, they might have been left wet and hung up to dry. I was unfortunate enough to have the knowledge of my brother being built like a damn Tic Tac, and although I hadn't seen the guy fuck, there was only so much maneuvering you could do with such a tiny little dick and massive balls.

"Where's Sac?" I asked, noticing he wasn't around as I took another mouthful from the bottle and gritted my teeth as the Seven scorched my throat.

"Setting up the deal," Ghoul and Circuit said in unison.

"That fucker? What the hell, Ghoul? First, you send Diablo with me, and then you put Sac as the middleman." I was overstepping and I knew it, but someone needed to question Ghoul right now. As the Vice President of our chapter, I had to keep this motherfucker in check every now and then. I was the only person in the club who he listened to…sometimes. It depended on the day and whether he wore his emotions on his sleeve or not on how the conversation would go. Again, it was what we did for each other, so I wouldn't be backing down from this or anything else as crucial.

"What can I say?" he grunted. "Every brother needs to get their dick wet and commit their felonies somehow." He shrugged, opening his hand as Circuit sliced a couple inches off a straw, and dropped the new tooter he made into his palm. He was right, we all had to get experience when we could, but I wish he didn't gamble on the club's well-being when it wasn't necessary. I was overprotective and at times a downright asshole when it came to things associated with the club, but it had a lot to do with me having a type-A personality.

We all had our vices. Mine was whiskey and used to be nicotine, and Ghoul, well, Ghoul's was coke. We were all trying our damnedest to forget something, and although I didn't particularly agree with his choice of poison, I wasn't one to judge it too much either. It didn't matter what way we chose to drown our sins, we all fought to suffocate our demons the best we could.

"Toot toot, mother fuckers. Fucking hookers and cocaine, just trying to live my best life." Ghoul chuckled, lifting his face off the bar and pulled the tooter from his nostril, chucking it into a nearby empty ashtray.

"Hell, yeah," Circuit cheered pouring a shot for Ghoul and the rest of us, grabbing his and holding it high in the air. "To living our best life. Forever Bastards, and Bastards forever," he yelled, and the rest of us brothers joined him in the chant before flipping our shot into the back of our throats.

5
RAY

What was I doing with my life? It was an issue I faced each day as I laid in bed and then begrudgingly forced myself to rise out of it. Some days were harder than others, but I tried to remember this wasn't what dad would want for me. It wasn't what I wanted for myself either, but my self-preservation wasn't exactly at a high point right now. For the first few days, I didn't make it further than the bathroom and when absolutely necessary, down to the kitchen for food. Even though I didn't have an appetite, I generally pushed something into my body, understanding I had to be semi-healthy to take care of Mom. I'd promised to essentially take Dad's place, so that required being here, even if each time my lungs flattened upon exhalation, the wish for death tried a little more to overpower me.

I missed my dad so much, it physically hurt. I didn't know until he passed that sadness could be something tangible. It was an emotion everyone person was capable of, only some chose to fight it, while others wallowed in the depths of its tides. At least that was how I thought people dealt with the emotion before we lost Dad. I was noticeably wrong all those years; it wasn't a choice at all. On occasion, people were just sad. That fact didn't change because a person willed it to be so. It was putting a boat into capricious waters on a clear day, only to capsize minutes later by the white caps that emerged unexpectedly. A person couldn't prepare for true, gut-wrenching misery. It was abrupt and tended to overstay its welcome in their life.

I'd wake from happy dreams of things that happened during my childhood, like when Dad taught me how to bait a hook, only to wake up with the stupid fucking knowledge that he was no longer here. Other times, I had nightmares of him being trapped, and I couldn't save him. It didn't matter what my subconscious chose to slap on the projector at night, eventually, my heart always broke all over again. It was as if each day, I lost him for the first time, and my heart was bound with such power that each constriction brought more anguish than the earlier one. All I wanted to do was lay on the mattress and waste away. I really had no purpose.

It'd been two weeks since Dad's funeral, and the highlight of my days was playing scrabble with the next-door neighbor, Mrs. Flowers. I was going stir-crazy and had to do something to occupy my wandering mind, so board games with her was better than merely doing nothing to pass my time. It was a very welcomed distraction that kept me busy and freed my mind from the treacherous cloud that begged to submerge me entirely into mourning. I couldn't give myself credit for the idea, she pushed it on me, offering to play every time she saw me. Eventually, I gave in to her plan and just let the rest of the world melt away. I should have been doing something more constructive with my time, like looking for a job, but I wasn't ready to reassemble all those broken pieces. My mind had filled with guilt after the funeral, and I knew right then, I wouldn't be breaking the promises I'd made Dad. Not only would I not move back to Kentucky, but I would also settle here for a while to keep my word to him. None of that would happen anytime soon, though. I simply couldn't go on pretending the world was the same without him because it wasn't, at least not for me. A very key part of my life was gone, and I didn't know how to fill the void.

Mom hadn't been home too much. She immersed herself in volunteer work at the hospital against my better judgment. Neither of us needed to be there; its halls were filled with the lingering ghost of Dad's memories. Nothing I said changed her mind, though; this was where she wanted to pass her time.

"Penis for the win," Mrs. Flowers chuckled as she dropped the letters one wooden tile at a time onto the board. My mouth fell open, and I didn't bother looking at the letters she'd played at all.

"I can't..."

"Good grief, girl. I said penis. I didn't say dick." She shook her head and took a sip from her cup, which I was questioning if it actually contained tea as she had said. My nostrils flared as I inhaled, expecting to be knocked down with the scent of liquor, and my curiosity piqued when I didn't find it.

My entire childhood was filled with memories of Mrs. Flowers, none of which had she ever said anything remotely close to anything she had today. Baking cookies or patching up my scrapes and scratches with a Snoopy band-aid, yes, those were the things I remembered. Yet, when she said penis and then dick, I couldn't help except wonder what she said when I hadn't heard her.

"Rachel, you're old enough to hear these words." She set her teacup onto the wobbly table beside the game board and crossed her legs. I nodded in response unable to muster much more of a reply.

"Please tell me this isn't the first time you've heard them." She smirked and lifted her mocha-colored hand to her face, trying to hide her amusement. "Do we need to have the talk? Girl, I can tell you some stories. Speaking of..." She held up one finger and pulled a book from the shelf of the table. "Here. This will do the explaining for me and then some."

My eyes roamed the very familiar cover of the paperback copy of an erotic novel, and I stifled the giggles boiling out of my body. I had read the entire series at least five times and could probably quote more excerpts than most. I'd been an avid romance reader since the ripe age of thirteen, and from there, I spiraled into the erotica genre several years later.

"Just read it, okay?"

I rolled my shoulders and bit my lip, trying to gain some semblance of composure before I nodded in agreement. The thought of her reading books in this category both made me question a lot of things she'd said to me during my childhood and appreciate them a lot more. She had dropped hints about sex all through my teenage years, and I'd often asked myself if they had a hidden innuendo but shut those thoughts down fast. It was Mrs. Flowers for crying out loud. Apparently, I had been right all along. She was a dirty old woman and wasn't as innocent as I believed. I guess she figured I was older and there was little point to hide anything from me now.

"Thank you," I politely said, shoving the book underneath my arm as I stood to excuse myself.

"Leaving already?"

"I have some reading to do, right?"

"Yes. Educate yourself, and maybe the next game, you won't choke when I play the one-eyed snake."

I plugged one ear and then the other with the tip of one of my fingers, wondering if I had actually heard her correctly. "Doubtful," I barely spat out of my lips and ran toward Mom and Dad's house in shock, my body teetering on exploding with laughter and assuming a fetal position with the new knowledge I'd been given. I didn't look back at her to see her reaction because I couldn't. She had a wonderful sense of humor, this much I was aware of, but apparently, I had only scratched the surface.

6

RAY

"Enough is enough, Ray. You're getting out of bed today." Mom sniffed and wrinkled her nose as she pulled the cover off of my head and bent to kiss me on the forehead. "I miss him, too, but we both have to keep going...and showering. You need to shower."

"Why don't you tell me how you really feel, Mom?" A small chuckle traveled through my body and snuck out of my mouth. I didn't want to laugh because any time I did, it felt like I was enjoying the world when I didn't deserve to or have the desire to do it. Various people dealt with death differently. If I could choose, it would be to avoid the whole process entirely. If someone were to place me in one of the stages of grieving, it would be denial, but that would mean I hadn't accepted Dad was gone. I had, so who could say where I was? Instead of avoiding the stages of grief as I wished, I was experiencing all of them together. Really, where I landed in the mix of it all didn't matter. The one thing I was certain of, I fucking hated every minute of it. I never realized how easy it was to succumb to the poison of depression. People often talk about those who didn't do much outside of lay in the bed and wallow in their thoughts, I too was someone who was quick to judge another who did this in the past, but that was before I experienced it...before I understood.

I had always tried to keep an open mind before, yet when it came to someone in a similar predicament, I sounded a bit like a broken record. *"C'mon, why don't you get out of the bed? You know there are things outside waiting for you."* Honestly, I couldn't remember exactly what I said, but it was something like that. I was an idiot with shitty offers to someone who needed a monumental thing to move them. I didn't realize that no matter how much someone else wanted something for you, it might not be enough. Depression and anxiety were monstrous opponents. When you thought you had the upper hand, one or both of them opened their Trojan horse, and a new wave of fear knocked you backward.

"I'll shower tomorrow, Mom, I promise." I stole the comforter from her grasp, rolling away from her, and groaned as I wrapped my body into a blanket burrito.

"No, you'll shower today," she ordered in a stern voice that had a hint of humor to it.

"Tomor—" had barely left my lips as the sound of her shuffling something stopped the word from finishing. "Okay. I'll shower today," I spat out in a hurry, untangling myself from the cover and got to my feet as fast as I could. If she wasn't my mom, I wouldn't have known what she was about to do. Maybe, if I wasn't her kid, she would have never started it to begin with. I had always been a person who was hard to wake up. The earlier in the day anyone tried, the harder it was. Hell, I set at least ten alarms on my cellphone each morning before work.

"I can't believe you were going to pour water on me," I said with a roll of my eyes. "I'm not a teenager anymore."

"Then quit acting like one and go wash your ass."

Again, another chuckle floated from my body, and I shook my head. She wasn't backing down from this, and she had a point. I lifted my arm and was almost knocked down with the proof. "Fine," I simply answered, stripping my shirt off and throwing it into the laundry basket beside the door.

"I'm going into town today with Wren. We're going to get our nails done," Mom called through the door and opened it as soon as I closed it. "Do you want to go?"

"Thank you, but no thank you."

"Maybe next time. Love you," she suggested in a voice full of disappointment as she kissed me on the cheek, and I did the same to her.

"Love you, Mom. Next time, I'll go. Promise. That shit is horrible for your nails, you know that, right?" I wasn't sure at what point in this entire debacle I began lying to my mom, but each one came easier than the last. I told myself it was what was best for her healing process, and I'd figure out mine later. I refused to give myself a timeline because I didn't see an end in sight. I felt like a complete asshole for not bouncing back and being there for mom in the ways I should be, but I never expected this to be as hard as it was.

When Wren and I were younger, a day at the nail salon followed with dinner and a movie was something we always did with our moms. After I moved and started working in the hospital, I wasn't allowed to have acrylic nails—it was an infection control thing. It wasn't until I actually gave my nails a break that I realized how much damage applying fake nails did to my natural ones. I used that as an excuse now, and I knew it, but it was the only feasible one I could think of.

She frowned and silently shook her head. "Might be, but they look nice." She clicked her nails on the door, letting them disappear one at a time with her and closed the door behind her.

I loved my mom for all she was doing and what she wasn't. A few weeks had passed, and it took until today for her to get back to her pushy self. Dad was no longer here to act as a buffer between us, therefore, from now on, it would be us raw and unfiltered. The reason we clashed as much as we did wasn't that we were so different we couldn't get along, it was that we were more alike than either of us would admit out loud. Of course, I had gotten a good portion of my personality from Dad, but the strongest parts came from Mom. Now, we were two very opinionated, headstrong women living under one roof again. I bet Dad was laughing his ass off wherever he was. I hadn't decided what I believed about where people went or did in the afterlife, ergo I couldn't begin to guess where his spirit was or if he had one flying about in the first place.

As early as she woke me up, I thought for sure Mom and Wren would catch a matinee and a quick lunch, and Mom would be home by now. When five came around, it was obvious I was wrong. The hour between five and six ticked by agonizingly slow, and I considered crawling back into bed. The only thing that stopped me from doing so was knowing that if she came home and I was laying down again, she would use the bucket of water she almost threw this morning.

By six-thirty, I decided to go out on the back deck and swing. Mom and Dad's house wasn't in the heart of Cleveland, it was tucked away in the rural area of Cuyahoga County. It was close enough that driving to the city wasn't a pain in the ass, but far enough away that it was peaceful. When a lot of people who had never been to Cleveland thought of it, they immediately connected it with the medical field, considering the large hospital here. They were rarely aware of the beautiful countryside where I had grown from a child to an adult. When people living in Kentucky found out where I was from, they automatically asked about the city. It never included the peacefulness of fishing off a dock or watching wildlife from a porch, both things I loved about this area.

The breeze swirling around me was warm but had a slight whisper of dampness in its breath. I deeply inhaled as much of it as I could into my body and smiled. The smell of rain was one of my favorite things in the world. There was nothing like it. It was the serenity that flowed through the world before the clouds burst open and rain fell from the heavens. Not even meteorologists could quite pinpoint what a storm would do, they had a good idea but had no way of being one hundred percent certain. Nature was volatile, and I loved it for that very reason. It made me crazy, but I didn't like things to be predictable. It was when I could guess every movement before it was made that I lost interest in a subject. I wanted to be shocked and living a life worthwhile, not mindlessly shuffling along from day-to-day.

That was one area Logan always surpassed any other man I met—not that there really had been someone else important because there hadn't been. Maybe that was the reason I compared all men to Logan, not ever giving the others a chance to win my heart. Perhaps, I would constantly do so merely because I had nothing else to compare. Who knew? Life with him was exciting, and I didn't know from one second to the next what we would be doing. At this moment, I allowed myself to admit I missed that part of him and nothing else. It couldn't hurt to open that door a tiny crack, right? As long as I didn't leave it open wide to let all the old feelings rush back in, I didn't think it could cause too much damage. So, I unlocked that part of my life and invited a tiny glimmer of light into the thoughts I'd buried deep within myself so many years ago. The door was only open for a second, and then I forced myself to think of something else. Anything that didn't involve him. The problem was, once I started thinking of him, I couldn't stop. I was such a fucking dumbass; there was a reason I didn't ask Wren about her brother.

Pissed at myself, I uncrossed my legs and jumped off the swing, grabbing a towel off the banister, not caring if it was even clean. There was one thing I could do to drown out the thoughts, and if I had to, so be it.

I was terrified of deep water. Even though I chased the unstable things in the world, I feared the unknown. It made absolutely no sense, but the truth was, I couldn't shake the fear of what laid below its surface, which was why it usually took a Xanax or a few shots to get me in that shit. However, Dad was a huge believer in facing one's fears, and being his child, he instilled that into me. A lot of times when I didn't want that value to be a part of me. It was ironic, whenever I wanted to clear my head, all I had to do was swim away from the shallows. Maybe it was simply that my fear and need to survive overshadowed any other thoughts attempting to travel through my head. I really never figured it out, and I didn't give a damn about thinking about it anymore.

It wasn't that Logan and I ended on bad terms—we didn't necessarily—In my opinion, it was worse because we never really had an ending, didn't have a chance to scream or cuss at each other. It was as if we were a fire that burned strongly one minute, and the next, a gust of air blew through with such strength, we were scattered too far to reach one another again, unable to rekindle our heat. All the pieces were still there, the embers lightly glowing, but ultimately, that too lost its luster.

Once I reached the spot my toes couldn't touch, I lifted my feet, and the water surrounded my head. When I spread my arms away from my body and panic thrummed through me, I was reminded that this was probably one of the stupider ideas I had come up with. Was it actually a bad thing that I thought of Logan? The answer was yes. I couldn't fall down that rabbit hole again. My mind was already so fucked, adding one more component into the mix, might push me over the edge. I wasn't taking care of Mom as I should've been; hell, I didn't really even care much for myself. I hated that I'd become a stigma of what a daughter did after a parent died. I wished for strength as I closed my eyes and let the water support my body. I didn't want to be like this forever, in a constant halt, but once my life stilled, I didn't know how to find my way back to movement again.

7

CROW

I'D SEEN MARY IN TOWN IN PASSING BUT HADN'T GOTTEN TO carry on what one would describe as a meaningful conversation. Ray was never with her, so maybe, she'd moved back to Kentucky.

I was curious, and the obvious way to get answers would be to ask my sister, Wren, but that would mean admitting she was right. She'd dangled her continued friendship with Ray in front of my face for years, waiting for me to crack and tell her I regretted not moving. Parts of me did think I was a dumbass for letting Ray go so easily, but others were happy I still called Cleveland my home—mainly the portions bursting at the seams with satisfaction that I was a Royal Bastard in this chapter. It was something that gave me pride because even though we did a fair amount of shady shit, we also did things for the community, too. Things that helped our household out when I was little like our annual toy drive. There were countless Christmases Mom brought us to the event, and the toy the brothers gave us was the only one we got that year. The club did these things to help out, but it didn't hurt that charity events were one of many unspoken reminders for the town of all the good we did. It helped them to turn a blind eye when we did illegal stuff because everyone had a little bad in them, right? No one was one-hundred-percent good, not even the best of people. My measurements leaned more toward the bad and horrific side of the scale, but I still had my morals that kept me from completely toppling over into Hell. In cartoons, the characters always had a tiny angel and devil sitting on each of their shoulders who helped them remain moral. I really thought both of mine wore horns, but on occasion, they decided it was best to take the high road when making decisions. Who the fuck knew?

"Give me two of the Boston creams, three with sprinkles, four glaze, and three blueberries," I called out the order to the young girl behind the counter as her eyes roamed my body from the floor to my chest.

"Ah. Yeah. Okay. You got it," she stammered, pinching the tongs and filling the box with the doughnuts one at a time. The barely legal girl batted her eyelashes, giving me what I could only assume to be her best attempt at a seductive look. I smiled respectfully trying not to completely crush her, but I didn't want to give her false hope either. I wasn't here to chase tail; I was here only to pick up a peace offering for Mary and get the fuck out. That was the plan before this random girl who was maybe in her early twenties crossed my path...technically, I guess I was in her way, but it didn't matter. I definitely was getting out of the door as quick as I came through it now. Most of the guys didn't care if a piece of ass was questionably eighteen or older, I did. It had always been one of my pet peeves.

"I'm taking this to my ex's house. She likes the glazed kind," I told her a white-lie, hoping she would get the point without me having to actually spell it out for her. I was technically taking them to Ray's house, it just wasn't the one where she currently lived. She used to like the glazed ones, which definitely wasn't the reason I bought four as if I was wishing to see her. I liked them, too. At least, that was what I told myself because fuck, I didn't want to go there with expectations.

"You know, most people are ex's for a reason, right?" She pouted, pursing her lips outward and watched me as she stood closing the box. Not that I was entertaining the idea, because I wasn't, but if I were thinking about it, I definitely wouldn't be now. I hated how some people automatically thought they shouldn't have to put any effort into getting things. Truthfully, the attitude as a whole pissed me off.

"That's what people say," I barked a little more aggressively than I had intended and paid for the doughnuts as quickly as I could.

Mary mentioned she wouldn't be volunteering anywhere today and should be home if I wanted to drop by. I took that as her way of politely telling me to get my ass to her house, and when her eyebrows pulled together, she made it pretty clear I shouldn't have waited this long to do so. She loved sweets, therefore, going emptyhanded to her house, especially knowing she was pissed at me, would be colossally idiotic.

I killed the engine of my Harley and kicked the standout, carefully leaning the bike's weight on it. Even though kickstands had been supporting things for longer than I'd been living, I didn't trust it entirely. I was no physicist by any means, but such a tiny thing holding all that up was sketchy to me. There had to be a window of error, and I didn't want my bike in whatever small percentage of failure I didn't know. I couldn't afford another ride now or anytime soon. The truth was, Ghoul helped me fix one of his old bikes, and I eventually bought it off him in order to have something to ride. To be a brother, you had to have a bike, that was common sense. A person couldn't be a biker without a bike. There were special cases, like Spider, the old fucker wasn't able to ride anymore, but he was still our brother. Hell, he was one of the original members of our chapter, and there was never a question of removing him when his arthritis got so bad he couldn't straddle a motorcycle anymore. Whenever we had church or parties, we all took turns taking a cage to go get him and made sure he was in attendance. Ghoul enforced this rule, which was one on a shortlist that he did. Anyone that Ghoul personally brought into the club held a special place with him. I was one of those brothers.

I took over Dad's shop a year before he passed away, and it was the reason I stayed in Ohio not chasing Ray and her dream in Kentucky. Someone had to run the family business, and being that I was the only child remotely interested, it fell to me. Honestly, I was lucky it did. We didn't have the money for me to go to college, and my grades were just below the required level of receiving scholarships. Of course, I could have gotten grants of some type, if I wanted to get technical, but I really didn't want to do anything other than work on vehicles. I loved taking things apart and putting them back together as did Ray. She tried her damnedest to get me to enroll in electrical engineering with her, saying it was basically like being a mechanic to machines. The thing was, I didn't want to work on high-tech shit, I liked the simplicity of cars and trucks. With them, there weren't as many surprises. They all needed their oil and tires changed eventually, and for me, that meant money in my pocket. Well, that was excluding the newer models of electronic cars, those things were foreign to me. I didn't know the first damn thing about them, but lucky for me, most people who lived around here couldn't afford them. If they could, they sure as shit didn't bring them to my shop.

The shop was actually how Ghoul and I met. He rolled up in a mint condition 1969 Pontiac Trans Am, and man, fuck, that thing was sexy. I whistled when he stepped out of it, which earned a very warranted concerning look from him. The whistle was for the car, not him. "Did you wash that motherfucker in a fresh coat of paint?" I said laughing. "That sweet ass car can't need much. What can we do for you today?"

"Nothing today," he said. "Just wanted to see that I'd be welcome when I did."

I smiled and threw him a business card. "Pal, you could fuck my old lady in my own house, and I'd still take care of that ride." He laughed and shook my hand, and we'd been friends ever since.

IMMEDIATELY, a new Buick in the nearby driveway caught my attention. Without question, it was Ray's. While I hadn't asked much about her, Wren liked to drop hints and keep me updated on the little things in Ray's life. *Fuck!* She wasn't in Kentucky as I had stupidly predicted. To make shitty beginnings worse, I hadn't fully thought out the plan of buying doughnuts instead of a fucking sealed box of chocolates. They were all smushed together, and a big part of the glaze was at the bottom of the bag. Saddlebags weren't exactly designed to hold a box of doughnuts.

"Fuck me," I complained a little too loud and wiped the glaze off my fingers and onto my blue jeans.

"Logan Williams, I will not do such a thing," a familiar voice answered, and I jumped at the sound.

"Mrs. Flowers? Damn it, sweetheart, I didn't know you were still alive," I joked, recognizing the calming tone that flooded a large number of memories from my youth.

"Don't act like you didn't see me just last Tuesday. You know damn well where I live, and if you came around more, you would know I hadn't keeled over yet." She tipped her nose downward and glared at me over her bifocals. "You used to like us." She released the screen door from her hand, and it clattered against the wooden door frame.

"Still do."

"Poor way of showing it," she called me on my shit, both of us knowing I hadn't visited here in quite a while. It was too easy to go on with your daily life and forget those who you didn't see on a daily basis. It was something people rarely gave thought to, unless of course in situations such as this.

"You're right. I'm a shit, but I'm your shit, and the only shit that you'll laugh and smile at when you step on it." I smiled meeting her at the bottom of her steps. "Doughnut?"

"We both know those aren't for me, but I'm going to take one anyway."

"Go ahead."

She grabbed one and nudged her head toward the house across the field...Ray's house. "Now, go on. Take that girl some happiness. She could use it."

I wanted to argue with her, but just like any other time, there wasn't any point. Mrs. Flowers always had called me on my shit, and truthfully, it was refreshing to see that fact hadn't changed. In a world that was constantly altering every second, it was nice to know some things remained untouched.

    I was nervous as fuck at the possibility of seeing Ray. It'd been years and much had changed, but in the same measure, not a lot had. I was balls deep in the club; it was my life. I didn't make any decision without keeping my brothers in mind. The thing that hadn't been altered too much was that I still thought of her. I wasn't sure if that meant I missed her, or just the idea of having someone by my side. I guess now was as good of a time as any to find out that answer. The only thing I was convinced about was that I picked the wrong time to quit smoking cigarettes cold turkey. I never half-assed anything, and when I decided to do something, I was all in. Now, I wish I hadn't done it that way. I regretted it, that was for damn sure.

8

CROW

I practiced what I would say to her as I paced back and forth on their porch. This shouldn't be this damn hard. We didn't owe anything to each other, but for some reason, I felt the need to explain to her why I quit calling. I didn't have a reason; we both were guilty of that and traveling to see each other. Society might say I regretted it, but what the hell did those assholes know anyway? Those shits used to think the world was flat, plus, I didn't owe them anything either. *Fuck!* This was stupid. I could bag a club skank and not once had my confidence faltered like it did with Ray.

"Fuck," a female voice shouted, and the bushes at the corner of the porch shook.

"Ray?"

"Yeah?"

"What the fuck are you doing in the bush?" I asked setting the box of doughnuts on the porch, something I couldn't do at home because Bologna, my dog, would have tackled the shit as soon as it was out of my hands. Thankfully, Wren was keeping him for the time being. She always did during this time of year since he was too big to throw on the back of my Harley, and I wasn't home enough to take care of him.

"Well, I...I'm stuck."

I crept down the stairs and to the bush. This, I had to see for myself. She was drenched from head to toe, and somehow, a branch was strung through a belt loop of her jeans. A smile pulled at my lips, and before I knew it, my sides heaved with silent laughter. It didn't take any time for the silence to find volume and my stomach to ache from how hard I was laughing. "How in the hell did you manage this?" I spat out in between chuckles, trying to catch my breath.

"Quit being a shit, Logan! Fucking help me," she groused and tried to kick me with her left foot, but I wasn't remotely close enough for her to do so. Hearing her say my name was a surreal moment. I'd missed her voice, and I wasn't aware of it until this moment. I used to love it when she said my name, regardless of the emotion behind it.

"Logan, seriously!" She wiggled her ass. The bush shook, a few leaves falling on her face, and she glared at them and then me.

"Alright, fine. You don't have to be a drama queen." I snickered once more, grabbing the limb in both of my palms and snapping it to free her.

"We both know I'm not a drama queen." She straightened her legs, brushing random leaves off her soaked clothes and pulled at her shirt that clung to her body. Now that I could actually see her, all of her, my mouth watered at the sight. She was the same girl I loved so many years ago, but the world had seasoned her into a beautiful woman. Her hair was long and brown the last time I saw her, but now, it was short and a pinkish-red color. I'd seen the color on a few women around the club and hated it, but on her, it was fucking sexy as hell. She had a little more ink than the last time we saw one another, and I didn't know who her artist was, but damn, they had done an excellent job. Really, given the canvas, someone couldn't fuck up a tattoo too much. Anything would look gorgeous on her skin.

"I'm not," she whined, her deep brown eyes searing me with a storm of emotions.

"You're not," I mechanically repeated, my eyes glued to hers as I offered my hand to help her off the ground.

She sucked in a hesitant breath and chewed on the corner of her mouth as if trying to decide if she should accept my assistance or deny it. She slowly placed her palm in mine, and it was like fucking wildfire spread throughout my entire body. I don't think I'd ever been so turned on by such a tiny gesture. Ray didn't trust easily, and I knew without a shadow of a doubt, she wouldn't put her faith in me ever again. I'd never been so happy to be wrong.

My dick throbbed with desire, and my balls ached with need. This was bad, and I couldn't deny it, but I didn't want it to stop either. I drank the fucking Kool-Aid her body offered me and was thirsty for more.

"So...what are you doing here?" Her eyes roamed over my face before flashing to our joined hands, and she jerked away from me, brushing her fingers through her hair.

"Why are you all wet?" I barely managed to say, and both of us froze. The exchange between us was excruciating. If she were anyone else, I would take her inside and fuck her brains out, but she wasn't. She was her, and I was me. Too much history preceded today, and along with that came hurt feelings and unspoken words.

"Umm. So, how about those Browns?" She changed the subject as fast as she could and walked around the porch and up the stairs.

"I fucking hate sports."

"I know. So do I."

"Then why bring them up?" I probed and bent to pick up the box of doughnuts, opening the lid and pushing them in her direction. "Doughnut?"

"Why buy three glazed?" She immediately rebounded, grabbing one and lifting it to my mouth. I bit down on it, and she grabbed one for herself, taking a huge bite and then met my gaze. "Talking has never been our strong area, so let's skip it."

My eyebrows furrowed together, and just as I was about to protest, she spoke again, "Just for a little bit? From the look on your face and the amount of pacing you were doing, you hadn't planned on seeing me any more than I did you. Let's eat these and then we can talk. Okay?"

I slowly nodded and curled my tongue around the doughnut in my mouth—it almost dropped out—until we were inside and I set the box down to grab it.

"Okay." I agreed, but really, I had no fucking clue what I had consented to do.

9

RAY

WHAT IN THE ACTUAL FUCK WERE WE DOING? This was awkward. Every time I wanted to walk away, my stupid mouth opened on its own again. When I wanted nothing more than to be alone, I invited him inside. When I went to change my clothes, I told him to find us something to drink. It was as if my body was on autopilot and my mouth was driving the whole damn thing, my brain and wants took a backseat on this ride.

I figured things would have changed given the amount of time that had passed since we last saw one another, but if anything, things had intensified for me. The moment I saw him, I hid in the bush. As I did, I was more than aware it was a childish response, but I wasn't ready to see him. Not yet. The thing about life was, it didn't matter if you were prepared, it just happened.

Logan was the same person I left seven years ago, yet, in the same measure, he was very different. His facial hair had grown, and he had a couple of new tattoos under his leather vest, but that wasn't the first thing I noticed. The way he proudly carried his shoulders pinned back and the way he constantly looked around like a snake ready to strike was new. Logan had never been what one would consider a "free-spirit", in fact, he was borderline OCD with certain things, but this wasn't a part of that. The world had aged him, and honestly, I didn't know how. I wanted to, though. This was the reason I didn't want to see him because when it came to him, my curiosity was never-ending...among other things of course.

I finished the last piece of the third doughnut and sipped on the coffee Logan had made us, realizing the whole no conversation between us was coming to a head. It was a waiting game to see who broke first. We both used to be stubborn as hell, and I was sure that fact hadn't waivered for either of us. It certainly hadn't for me, otherwise, I wouldn't keep stuffing sweets in my mouth to prevent us from talking. It was as if the moment I saw him standing on the porch, all rational thoughts escaped me. I reverted back to the girl who left him behind; somehow, it was like I was no longer a woman and like the past didn't happen. It had, though. We'd both assessed our priorities, and we weren't number one on each other's list—that gutted me, and I knew it did him, too. Life was shitty like that. If it weren't for responsibilities, we would have gone on undamaged by the pressures of the world.

"You want another?" he asked, his interest piqued and his eyes wide. He recognized what I was doing: avoiding him. Of course, he did. I wished I wasn't this transparent, but when you spend the majority of your life with someone, they figured you out, even down to the weirdest habits. This was one of mine; I hated talking about things when they didn't have a resolution in sight. It was something he and I used to share, and based on the way he was shoving food in his mouth as fast as I was, he more than likely still felt the same. We were both problem solvers—it irked the shit out of me to fail in finding a solution. Perhaps that was the easiest way to describe what happened between the two of us; there wasn't an easy answer. Hell, there wasn't even a slightly difficult one to find, so we didn't. We both gave enough to say we tried, but we didn't, not really. I'd seen people who tried. They fought for what they had and refused to let it go, that wasn't what we did.

I slowly shook my head, mulling over my recent thoughts. I'd spent so many years avoiding him when, in reality, it seemed pointless to do so. Was I hurt? Sure, but he was, too. I bit the corner of my mouth and released my lip with a pop. I was tired of only partially living my own life. Maybe, had I not been such a shit, I would have come home and been able to spend more time with Dad, I would have known he was sick long before it was too late. The what-ifs were enough to drive me insane, so I simply decided I wouldn't let them anymore. At least not today. Tomorrow was another story.

"Do you ever wonder..." My voice trailed off, suddenly my bravery back-stepped, and I questioned myself.

"What would have happened if we stayed together?" He finished my thought and patted the couch cushion beside him. I joined him, nodding in agreement. "Me too. All the fucking time, which I wouldn't accept the truth myself, but I'll admit it to you." He ran his hands through his hair, rubbing the back of his neck a few times before continuing, "Really, Ray, who the fuck knows? It doesn't change anything, right?" He brushed his index and middle finger over his mouth a few times before cupping his lips and letting them go.

"Guess not. We can't fix the past," I pointed out, more to myself than to him.

"Can't run from the future either." He half-heartedly smiled, leaning his head against the back of the couch, a whirlwind of emotions stirred behind his irises, and his pupils broadened. My pulse quickened the longer I watched him watching me. One of us should say something else, but what was there to say? Should I scream that I'd missed him every day since we last saw one another? No. That would be a huge mistake; I wasn't even sure if that was what I truly felt or if it was simply being in such close proximity to him that confused my senses.

My body reacted to his as it had in the past, making me ache for him to touch me, but again, that would certainly be another misstep. I needed to move from this couch, however, I didn't want to all at the same time. I'd never been one to look for grand gestures from a higher power, and yet, I needed an intervention. Being around Logan was intoxicating and despite how confused I was, one thing was clear: I'd missed him.

10

CROW

I told myself to get away from her, but my body didn't listen. In fact, the fucker scooted closer and brushed her hair out of her face, my hand then rested on her collarbone. This was bad, I would ruin her. I didn't have promises of eternity to make to her, and honestly, I wasn't sure if that was what I wanted to do anyway. I liked her being around, but my life wasn't as simplistic as it was when we'd parted. It wasn't only me now. I had a shop, which practically ran itself, and was VP of our chapter. There was a long list of felonies that might eventually catch up with me, and she didn't need that bringing her down. There wasn't a question in my mind that she didn't need to be tangled up in any of the shit I was.

Not to mention The Dogs were bound to retaliate, it was just a matter of when and where. Ghoul had called in a favor from our DC chapter, and a handful of brothers were to arrive in a few days to add to our security and back up our SGT at arms, Wily. He wasn't a huge guy, but the fucker was mean, which was how he earned his road name from Ghoul.

One look at him and Ghoul didn't think the guy had what it took to be a Bastard, fuck if he was ever wrong. Wily taught all of us that it was the little guys you had to worry about. What he didn't have in size, he more than made up for in aggression. One might say he had a Napoleon complex, but he wasn't short, just smaller than a lot of the brothers.

All of those reasons didn't stop me when they should have. Maybe this was what we needed, closure. Who the fuck knew? I fucking didn't. I was insane for even entertaining the idea of hooking up with her, but my dick had other plans, a course of his own.

Her eyelids slowly closed and reopened as my fingertips trailed up her neck, cupping her cheek. This was the moment my sins would seep so incredibly far beneath her skin that she could never erase them. My mind screamed for me to find the strength to stop what was happening between us, and then it implored me for the literal opposite. If this happened, my corruption would be a part of her life from this day forth. She didn't have the faintest clue of the wickedness I was capable of, but it was something I rarely forgot. My past was an atrocity that would stain her steps, lingering in her shadow, awaiting the day to rise from the ground and consume her life. Maybe I was being paranoid. It wasn't like I was asking her to marry me. This should be a simple situation to deal with. No decision involving Ray was an easy one to make, though. I constantly questioned if what I was doing was right or wrong. Most of the time I didn't find any more of an answer than when I had begun thinking about it.

I told myself I wouldn't initiate things between us, but I did anyway. Albeit, it was an involuntary move, one I was certain Mary and Wren had played a significant role in. Had it not been for Mary's guilt-tripping me, I wouldn't have dropped by the house unannounced. Regardless of what brought us together, I vowed to keep Ray safe, even if it was me I had to protect her from. I was bargaining, trying to justify the moment. If she was okay with it, I would be, too. Really, I had no idea what to do next. My body froze in place, I would not do this to her. I couldn't be selfish with her, no matter how much my body begged for it.

Her hands shook as they traveled up my chest, and I sucked in a long breath when her fingers touch my cut. My initial reaction was unstoppable, my hands flew up to hers, and caught them just as they reached my VP patch. It wasn't easy to let someone see me for who I really was inside. My colors were my protection, most people wouldn't come near me simply because I wore them. Ray wasn't most people, though. She may be the only person on this planet who knew the true me. I wasn't a lying son of a bitch, people got what they saw, but that didn't mean I was forthcoming with my innermost thoughts. Ray used to have a way of prying them from me without ever having to ask.

"Am I not supposed to touch it?" She withdrew her hand quickly and recoiled from me, wrapping her arms around her body. The light of desire swiftly evaporated from her irises and betrayal and hurt pulsated behind them. It was difficult watching her trust wilt into bitterness. I had to do something and fast.

Fuck! I didn't mean for this to happen. I'd told myself I tried to prevent it from moving forward, but I hadn't really. Never once had I given her the impression this was something I didn't think was a good idea. We had too much history to make it possible to easily walk away. I guess my subconscious was more ravenous than I was aware of. The only possibility left was to face the truth. This was never about closure for me as I thought, it was pouring salt directly into an oversized wound by the gallon and idly standing by while the pain swelled. If this was one night or forever, I would take it. It didn't matter how things ended with her as long as she was at peace with it. My feelings and what shape I was in after this no longer mattered. I would deal with my damage later, right now, I had to fix what I had already wrecked between us.

"Ray, I'm sorry," I took her cupped hands into mine and kissed the backs of them. "It's just hard for me to do this."

"Because it's me?" Her voice broke, and she stared at the only part of our bodies that touched. Our clasped hands.

"Well, no and yes," I honestly answered, and when she tried to pull away, my hold intensified. She needed to hear the rest of my statement before she made a decision. If she wished for me to walk out her door and didn't want to see me again after she heard what I had to say, I would honor it. I would hate every waking second I roamed this earth from that point on, knowing she was this close and I ruined us.

With a massive inhale and an enormous amount of courage, I continued, "Just let me finish, please. If I don't say it now, I won't. You know that's how I am."

"It's how you used to be."

"I haven't changed all that much, not really. I have a criminal record thicker than I care to admit, but I'm still me. It's not hard for me to be with you. I've thought of it for so long, I was pretty damn positive I imagined it at times," I paused, waiting for her to say something, but no sounds left her body. She pulled in a silent breath and the smallest amount of hurt faded from her body. Her shoulders relaxed and she shook her head. "It's the truth. But that isn't the part you need to hear. It's so fucking hard to be here with you again. I knew we would never see each other anymore, and if we did, it would be when you came back after you married some rich asshole I would hate from afar. I promised myself I wouldn't stand in the way of your future; I can't give you anything. I'm a fucking nobody. I mean, fuck, what do I have to offer?" Uncertainty rattled through my bones as the words came faster than I could process them.

"You're all I need right now, Logan. That's what you have to offer. You." She sighed and rubbed small circled onto my palms with the pad of her thumbs. "I regret so much of my life, and if I could have a redo, there's so much I would do differently...especially things between us. That's not possible, though. Is it?" She sniffed as her declaration overtook her and one singular tear snuck down her face. She rubbed her cheek against her shoulder, wiping the tear away and huffed, annoyed with herself. This was something a lot of people wouldn't give a second thought to, but Ray always hated letting people see her cry.

"We've sure fucked a lot up, haven't we?" I asked, trying to lighten the mood. It wasn't easy for either of us to face our past. Clearly, she regretted as much as I did. In the back of my mind, I always figured she did, but hearing her admit it, was different. My heart pounded apprehension with each beat, one second living in the moment, and the next thud, fell somewhere else in time as I thought of everything between us. The past, present, and future.

She faintly nodded, and I pulled her against me, hating it had taken such a long time for us to find each other again. No one had the power to predict how much shit we could have prevented had we both not been too stubborn to pick up a damn phone. All this time, I stayed away because I thought that was best for her. Hell, it was probably the most decent thing I would ever do in my life. It was the reason I didn't chase her; I saw how much I loved her and understood letting her go was the only selfless thing I could do at the time. The thing was, I wasn't a noble person, and I couldn't say with a great deal of confidence that I ever was. With her body against mine, I knew the answer, at least for now. I'd been in the darkness for so long without her, today, I would recklessly follow her into the light. Having her here didn't make me any less damned than I was yesterday, but there was one unquestionable fact. when I was with her, I wasn't as broken. At this moment, she quieted the frenzy of my tormented thoughts and silenced the demons within my mind with her mere presence. I had almost forgotten what it was like to be with her, the reason I didn't reach out to her when she quit calling. She had been my own personal form of compulsion and evidently still was. Some people injected drugs into their veins, while others lost themselves in the bottom of a bottle, pursuing comfort. For me, she was the only addiction I would always crave. I understood everything then: I would never get enough of her.

Our kiss was sudden, and I wasn't certain who kissed who first. The way our tongues demanded more from the other, it wasn't clear if this was reconnection or a goodbye. I pled with God not to let it be our last. We'd gone too many years without the other, and it was as if we were trying to make up for the time we missed.

I ripped my cut off and put it on the back of the couch, and she pulled her shirt off at the same time, flinging it across the room. Her lips branded me as hers, and I would claim her body as mine. When she breathed out, I breathed her in. The constant back and forth in my mind slowed with every touch between us.

She watched me through her thick eyelashes while she climbed onto her knees and stopped moving. It was almost like she was asking me what direction we were headed. I had absolutely no fucking clue and probably never would. The one undeniable reality was what I wouldn't admit to her. Not now and honestly I didn't know when I would, ergo I spoke with verity and hoped it was enough. "I missed you, Ray. So fucking much," I said in a thick voice, my fingertips pressing into her back, my thumbs hooking through the loops of her pants as I tugged her on top of me.

"I missed you more, Logan." She panted in between the words, grinding against me. I couldn't take anymore, and I didn't know if it was because of her words or the way her hips moved against mine. I had to get rid of our clothes and fast. Otherwise, she was about to be extremely disappointed.

Flipping the button of her jeans between my thumb and two fingers, I undid her pants and rushed to pull down the zipper. She lifted herself up, and I yanked the denim off her body as she raised her knees one at a time to help. My thumb went to work on her clit at once causing my dick to throb in agony. All I could think about was being inside her and how fucking hot she was.

Dropping onto my hand, she guided it to her entrance, pushing her lace panties to the side for better access. She directed two of my fingers inside her with a few of her own, and I gritted my teeth. At this rate, I would come before she had a chance to touch me. I had to pace myself because I would be damned if that happened. I was going to fuck her tonight, even if it killed me. There was no going back from this, I was seeing it through to the ending.

She pumped her pussy up and down the length of my fingers, and just as her walls clenched around them, she stopped to undo my blue jeans and circled her hand around my shaft. A pounding pulse vibrated up the length, and the head expanded a bit from the rush. A bead of liquid flowed down the top of my dick, and she flipped a finger up, oiling the engine, so to speak.

This was fucking torture. I'd thought I couldn't go any longer before, but now, I was at my breaking point. I wrapped my fingers around hers and cupped her ass with the opposite hand, steering her body toward my tip. When her clit touched it, we both moaned, and although I could look at her breathtaking body from now until the end of days, my eyes flickered to her warm honey eyes. I saw the emotion behind them and would bet the same was mirrored in mine, but I couldn't say the words. I was a fucking fool, and now more than ever, I wanted to say them, but I didn't know if she was ready to hear them. these words were the right ones to tell someone at the wrong moment, and I kept them to myself, basically repeating what I'd said earlier. "I missed you so fucking much, Ray," I was barely able to mumble in a voice full of desire for her.

"I know." She smirked, moving my tip slightly to touch the edge of her clit, and it was only then, I realized what she was doing: intentionally making me suffer. Any other time, I would have given just as much hell and afflicted just as much agonizing persecution because that was how we used to do things. Despite how much we wanted to cling to the people we used to be, we weren't those people. We were the same in many ways yet differed in so many more. The one factor that remained untouched was our profound need for each other.

I flicked my tip against her clit a few more times. When her breathing increased, I rocked into her. Her pussy was unbelievably tight, tighter than I remembered, as she sent pure bliss into my body. I answered by driving unbridled ecstasy into hers. I didn't know what tomorrow would hold, but tonight, it was just us. I refused to let anything else take center stage because she was my main focus, and I was hers. Neither of us found feasible answers for where we stood with one another, but we would unquestionably stand with each other to find the solution.

11

RAY

Hearing people call him Crow and not Logan would be bizarre, really fucking weird, honestly. We both agreed to dive into each other's world to see how things would go. It might be the ending we both sought after, or it could be a very peculiar beginning to something entirely different. Neither of us had any clue at all, but it got me out of bed today, so that was something.

"Here, put this on. Don't want to hurt that beautiful head of yours." Logan smiled, tossing a helmet to me and helping me hook it under my chin. He'd told me to wear boots, jeans, and layers because the ride from his house to the clubhouse—I think that's what Logan called it—might be cold. No one really could prepare for Ohio weather because it was unpredictable from one minute to the next. Thankfully, I could still fit into the clothes hanging in my closet that I'd left behind at Mom and Dad's. I appreciated the sentiment, so I didn't tell him it was pretty clear what I should wear, that would have made me look like an asshole. I merely told him thank you before we swung by last night to pick up a few things so I could stay the night at his house to make things go a little smoother. We both knew I hated mornings and would be more likely to actually go if he was there to keep my mind on course.

Mom was full of questions but seemed only partly committed when asking them. Something told me she had a part in this, but I couldn't prove it. Logan hadn't expected me to be home, believing Mom would be. In her defense, she had invited me to go out with her and Wren, but I'd declined. Perhaps she was giving me an out without actually telling me what she was doing. It was right up the lane of things she would do to try and fix things. She was naturally a nurturer, and her go-to was busying herself with caring for other people when she should be doing it for herself. I was supposed to be taking care of her, but I think it had somehow transformed into the reversal. She was looking out for me and taking Dad's death better than I was. Of course, she was. She saw it coming, and they waited until the last minute to bring me into the loop. A part of me wanted to hate my parents for not telling me, however, knowing my Mom and Dad, they didn't want me to worry until there was really something to be upset about.

"Wrap your hands around my waist and scoot—"

"I learned to ride when you did, Logan," I interrupted and straddled the Harley behind him. "It's been a while since I've ridden, but it isn't that hard to sit still." I linked my arms around his sides and cupped my hands together in front of his stomach, giggling a little at his reaction in the mirror.

His eyebrows rose, and he tilted his head to the side. "Oh, you're bad, huh?"

"That's right, buddy." I slid my sunglasses over my eyes and pulled the black and red handkerchief up over my face to keep the risk of windburn down as much as I could. "Are you bad like me?"

"You bet your fucking sweet ass I am," he gruffly said, plastering a devious smile across his face as the engine of the bike roared to life. "I'm the worst, a fucking nightmare."

I grinned wickedly behind the material and leaning forward to whisper into his ear as I got comfortable on the bike, "Depends on the judge."

It was nice to be on a bike again. It was something I hadn't realized I'd missed, but I did. After a while on the road, signs and trees all blurred together, blending into the background. My eyes became transfixed on the sky ahead of us as it pulled the sun into the horizon. Being on a motorcycle for a prolonged time was kind of like driving in a snowstorm, you didn't pay attention to the things around you, only the road ahead. This was much like the situation between Logan and me; we had tunnel vision and weren't giving any thought to the things around us. I hoped it didn't come back to bite us in the ass, but I didn't want to over-analyze anything. If I did, that meant this was more personal to me than it needed to be. We weren't putting a title on it, mostly because a status of "Who the fuck knows" didn't really roll of the tongue well for when nosey ass people would ask. Yet, with the exception of answering Mom, it would most likely be the answer I would give to people, either that or "Mind your damn business." I never claimed to be eloquent, there was a reason most of my co-workers had been male and not female. I often said things that didn't go over easily with others. Truthfully, I should come with my own warning label, but then again, people really should mind their damn business and tend to themselves. What was going on between Logan and me didn't concern anyone else, not that anybody had asked about it other than Mom.

Neither of us really gave her an answer simply glanced at each other and then shrugged our shoulders in agreement.

The trip was short...or long...frankly, I wasn't sure. I had lost track of time and wasn't paying attention to the duration. Logan parked his bike, and as soon as it was safe, I climbed off the back, groaning due to the pain in the middle of my spine as a result of sitting in one position too long. I guess that answered one thing, it wasn't a quick ride by any means. I stretched my arm above my head and pushed against my elbow with the opposite hand to force it a little further toward my shoulder, doing the same to the other side afterward. Logan was doing similar movements with his body, but they weren't as exaggerated. He obviously wasn't as bothered by the ride. Over the course of the last week, I'd only seen him drive his truck one time, and that was to go get some guy named Spider who I would apparently meet tonight.

There were a lot of guys dressed the same as Logan with black leather vests called "cuts" decorating most of their torsos; however, a small number of them wore blue jean cuts that had a "Prospect" patch on the upper right side of theirs. I didn't say much at first because I didn't understand all of the biker jargon they were using when talking to each other. Although I didn't know much about biker gangs, the one thing Logan made sure I did know was that the most important thing with them was having and giving respect.

"The fuck you been? Did you forget how a phone worked?" a loud voice boomed as soon as the door opened and Logan stepped inside. He led me by the hand into the clubhouse and stopped in front of the person I assumed owned the loud voice.

"This fucker here, this is Ghoul, our Prez," Logan introduced me to a bear of a man as we passed the pool table, and the stranger untangled his body from a redhead clinging to his side.

"The man," Ghoul waved his hand in front of his body, "The myth," he tapped the word President on the patch across his right chest wall, and finished, "The Legend—"

Logan grabbed Ghoul's hand before he could grab his junk, and Ghoul winked in my direction, his head falling back as a huge hoarse laugh filled the air. "You should see your fucking face, brother," he guffawed and pulled his hand from Logan's, holding it out for me to reciprocate. "It's a pleasure, young lady." He gave my hand a firm shake and clapped Logan on the back with his other.

"Don't get your panties in a fucking twist, Crow. Nobody is going to mess with your girl, you know that." He released my hand and nodded toward the bar, leading us through the crowded place. A ball of nerves swelled up into my throat, and I tried my best to force them down as I swallowed hard. Is that what I was now? His girl? I started to correct Ghoul but remembered what Logan had said about respect, especially to their President. He was the boss of the whole gang, and although Logan hadn't been too liberal with the details, he made sure I understood he wasn't someone to fuck with. He and Ghoul were close; he'd told me that much, but that wouldn't mean much if I straight up disrespected Ghoul in their house. This was their turf, not mine, so I did try to mind my p's and q's more than I normally would.

"Borrowed the panties from your drawer, Boss," Logan laughed as we three sat down on stools at the bar. It was nice to see Logan laid back. Well, as laid back as he could be, I guess. "Any updates from Heavy when they'll get here?"

Ghoul shot him a look and his eyebrows drew together. "I'm sure your lady...What's your name, sweetheart?"

"Ray."

"I'm sure Ray here doesn't want to hear shop talk. Let's save business for later; pleasure always comes first." He opened his hand and the guy behind the bar gave him a piece of a straw before Ghoul pulled a baggy from his shirt, pouring a little onto the woodgrain of the bar. I hadn't ever seen cocaine up close and personal, but I figured it was what the white powder was. "Want a toot?" he spoke to me, and I fought the urge to giggle out of nervousness. It made no sense, but when I was on edge, I tended to chuckle when other people talked to me.

"A toot?"

"You know, a snort, a line, a toot? Damn, Crow, I don't know where you got this one, but she needs some education," he joked and elbowed me in the side before sliding a straight razor out of his pocket and tapping the pile of drugs out into a line. "My name is Dr. Ghoul, and I'll be your drug instructor," a huge guffaw bellowed out of his throat, and he shook his head.

"Ghoul," Logan warned him.

"Crow." Ghoul met his gaze and obviously didn't give a shit. I didn't understand what words they were silently exchanging with me in the middle, but they didn't appear pleasant.

"Fucking hell, Crow, I'm just having a little fun, ain't that right, Ray?"

"Right," I answered, unsure if I was supposed to really answer him or not.

Logan leaned close to my ear and whispered at a volume no one else was able to hear, "You okay?"

A smile crept onto my lips, and my eyes flickered to Logan's, finding his filled with concern. He was trying to be protective and keep me safe, but the thing was, Ghoul reminded me of Randall, one of my old co-workers. They were both harmless in the sense, they didn't really mean half of what they said to me, or at least, I thought that was what Ghoul was doing. I could be completely wrong, and if I was, I would probably find out sooner rather than later. I hoped I was right, though. I hadn't really thought of my old co-workers since I came back to Ohio, I didn't think I'd had the time to, honestly. Yet, seeing the exchange between Logan and Ghoul, made me miss them and the constant back and forth shit we all gave one another.

"I'm good. I promise, Log—ow." I tried to call him Crow as soon as I remembered, but it didn't exactly work out.

"Fuck. See, she's good, Logow." Ghoul's eyebrows raised high on his forehead, and he slid a shot to me. "Ms. Ray and I are going to handle the pleasure portion while the rest of you fuckers talk business in the back," he said in a firm tone with a hint of humor. It was an order, but my guess was he was trying to keep the conversation light on my behalf.

12

CROW

"Heavy, the DC Prez, just called, they're hitting the road tomorrow. They're going to stay the night at Cyrus' clubhouse up in Pittsburgh then they'll be on the way here. Should put them in Cleveland sometime Wednesday, depending on how many stops they make," Wily said in a hushed tone after he shut the door behind him, his eyes shifting around the room to make sure we all were paying attention. We got a lead from an anonymous source The Dogs were going to retaliate—this much we expected. They didn't anticipate we would be ready, but this was our fucking town. The law was in our back pocket, and when they caught wind of something shady going down, they let us know. Truthfully, I think there was a pig in the doghouse because for the cops to have knowledge meant someone fucking squealed. For that alone, I would happily beat the fucking breaks off those guys. Add that to them trying to fuck us out of the AK deal, and those fuckers had a hell of a storm coming their way, and its name was the Royal Bastards.

"They bringing some girls?" Sledge asked, rubbing his

hands together. Our DC chapter was in the porn business, and we all knew it, but not all of our dicks had ears like Sledgehammer's did. Someone could simply whisper the word pussy and his dick got hard.

"I doubt it, this is a business trip," I paused, taking my normal seat at the table and scrubbed my palm over my face. "Is fucking all you think about, man?"

"Fuck. Ride. Sleep. Isn't that what we all do?"

"He has a point, Crow. What else do we do?" Circuit chimed in adding his two cents, which wasn't at all needed as he leaned his back against the wall, propping his left boot behind him for support.

"You fuckers are a bunch of dirty bikers." I tapped the table with the tip of my finger and closed my eyes for a second.

"So are you brother, that's why we let you stick around." Sleeper sat down beside me and waggled his eyebrows, both of us knowing that I've held a patch longer than he has.

"Matter at hand, what's the plan once they get here, Wily?"

"Heavy and the guys are going to stay around the clubhouse and make sure those fleabags don't try to come looking for the guns that aren't here anyway. Diablo, Sac?" he called their names to grab their attention.

"Brother?" They said in unison.

"No way of trailing those AK's back to us, right?"

"No fucking way, man. The law got their cut of the money, so even if someone did come snooping around, we have an alibi and the cops on our side," Sac assured in his usual laid-back voice. I wasn't sure how the fucker could function given the amount of weed he smoked on a daily basis, but it leveled him out. I saw him one damn time sober, and I hoped I never witness it again. I barely got a word in the conversation with him because he was talking so fast about nonsense. To be blunt, he reminded me of someone on crank—he was all twitchy and shit. If I didn't know he would never touch anything harder than weed, my money would have been on crystal.

"Ghoul know all of this?" I asked, concerned he wasn't in here and was out in the common area with Ray and Flashman. This was definitely a conversation he should be a part of.

"Yeah, he wanted us to fill you in," Diablo nonchalantly informed me, shoving a cigarette between his teeth and fishing a lighter out of his pocket.

"Everybody knew about this except me?"

"Ghoul tried to call you. Said you didn't answer. Probably just luck you are who you are, or you might be trading places behind the bar with Flashman." Diablo sucked on the end, and smoke bellowed down his body from his nostrils. Right now, Flashman was on Ghoul's shit list along with Circuit and Sledge. Circuit already did his time, and Sledge's was coming, but I could easily join them.

"He did mention that. My phone died." It was a rookie mistake, especially now, and although I couldn't stand Diablo most of the time, he was right. The stakes were high, and if anyone else had been unreachable when I tried to call them, I would be raising five levels of hell right now.

"Won't happen again, brothers," I promised. I would be the first to admit when I was wrong to people I cared about. I lived by the motto that you should be completely clear when it came to people who may be put in the position of saving your life or not. We were all Royal Bastards, and we lived by a creed and a set of bylaws, but that didn't mean a bad seed didn't come in under the radar every now and then. I wanted to make sure it that ever happened and we didn't catch it in time, maybe the fucker would remember my honesty and think twice before double-crossing me.

"How'd my boss treat ya?" I questioned Ray, noticing her glassy eyes.

"Perfect. The doctor is in." She laughed and turned toward Ghoul. "Ain't that right, doc?" A small giggle popped through her lips, and she nudged his shoulders with her own.

"That's right. Have you met my number one nurse, Crow?" Ghoul joked, catching her as she weaved on her barstool a bit. Rage, blind fucking rage was all I saw, but I reminded myself that she was her and he was him. Although she didn't have the word property slapped across her back, she was mine, and Ghoul wouldn't dare cross that line with me. I took a handful of cleansing breaths and resumed my seat at the bar beside Ray.

"Your girl is alright by me, brother. She can hold her whiskey and cusses like a fucking sailor. Why the fuck did you wait so long to bring her around? She's the little sister I never had." He laid it on thick after our eyes connected. Ghoul was more than aware I had a jealous streak a mile long; it was one of the reasons I never brought a girl to the clubhouse. The second was I hadn't had someone serious in my life since Ray. I guess I'd always been hung up on her even when she wasn't here.

I didn't have an answer for him, not one he wanted to hear anyway. If she'd never left...No. I wasn't spiraling down the same slope I had for so many years. We were trying to give us a shot, though I didn't know what target we were aiming at, and I needed to keep a clear mind to do so. All it would take was the smallest glimmer of negativity to drive all of this to shit. I refused to let it in. We'd spent so much time practically hating each other for letting everything fall apart, and I wouldn't do it this time.

"Yeah, she's pretty fucking awesome, isn't she, Ghoul?"

Ray smiled and slapped the bar. "Flashman, can I buy another round for the doctor and me?" I see she was introduced to him while I was in the back.

"This one is on me, Nurse." Flashman wickedly smiled, flaunting his perfect teeth. He was a pretty boy, definitely, someone most wouldn't picture when thinking about a biker. I hadn't when he walked through the club doors saying he wanted to prospect for the Royal Bastards. The thing was, the guy had a sinister streak; he liked blowing shit up. A pyro if I'd ever seen one.

"Thanks." She smirked and leaned her head onto my shoulder blade. "Thank you for this."

"For what?" I asked her, having no fucking clue what she was thanking me for.

"For helping me forget all the bad shit in the world."

When she said that, it fucking gutted me. I wanted to cradle her in my arms and never let her go. The truth was, I didn't know how many horrific things that were passing through her mind because she hadn't told me. It could have been because I didn't ask her. Yet, if I was being honest, even if I did, she probably wouldn't have told me. Ray wasn't one to slice her heart open and let the contents bleed out for everyone to see. She was more of a grin and bear it type of person. At least, she used to be.

"Thank you for being here with me," I voiced simply, my throat cracking. If I wasn't anything else, I tried to be truthful with everyone around me. My theory was, they could like me or hate me, but at least it would be the true person they formed their feelings about.

"Any time, Logan," she whispered.

"Boss, is it okay if we skip out?"

"As long as you promise to take good care of my nurse, then tires to the asphalt, brother," Ghoul reassured me, taking the last shot with Ray.

13

RAY

My head was dizzy from all the alcohol I'd consumed last night. I was compensating in liquor for what my body was screaming in nervousness. Once I hit my limit and I knew it, Ghoul still kept insisting we take another shot. I really liked that guy; he was an Ohio Randall if I ever met one. I could easily see him being someone I worked alongside.

My stomach churned, and I regretted drinking as much as I did last night, but at the same time, I didn't. It was the first time since Dad passed that I'd actually let loose. I yawned and stretched, opening my eyes, expecting to find Logan beside me. Instead, a white piece of paper on the nightstand greeted me.

Beautiful Nurse,
   Here's a couple Tylenol, you'll probably need them. I had to run to the clubhouse, but I'll be back before you know it. Make yourself at home. There's eggs in the fridge and frozen biscuits in the deep freeze, just pop

them in the oven at 375 for about fifteen minutes and they'll be done.

XO,

Logan

I smiled, thinking of all the years that brought us to this point. It was almost as if we had to lose one another to find each other again. This time would be different, I would be honest and upfront and demand the same from him. If our feelings were hurt by it, so be it. At least we would understand where we stood at the end of it.

I was afraid to say I had a new outlook today because anytime someone said that, something tragic happened. I wouldn't say I was hopeful because I didn't want to do that to us. We deserved a fighting chance. I flipped the white pills into my mouth and washed it down with the water Logan left for me, praying they kicked in quick. I hadn't had a hangover in some time, and this was a fucking powerful one.

Footsteps approached, and my body stilled in a half-awake, partially asleep stupor. The only other person who would be here would be Logan, so there was no need for alarm.

"Logan?" I called out through the house, just to settle my nerves a little, but there was no answer. I gathered the comforter around my body and made my way through his house to find him. "Don't be a shit. Answer me." Still no reply. I made it to the living room before I said anything again. "You're starting to freak me out! Answer me, Logan!" I insisted, my hands shaking with fear against my body.

"Your fuck boy isn't here, bitch," a man wearing a black ski mask said with delight, licking his lips and smacked a wooden baseball bat against his palm.

I ran as fast as my legs would carry me, clutching the blanket against my raging heart. All of a sudden, I came to an abrupt halt, and my feet flew out from under me. "I said stay put, bitch!" another voice violently shouted from behind me, and he yanked the blanket from my grasp. "Someone has to pay for the sins of the Bastards, and that someone is you."

Excruciating pain jolted from the back of my head to the front, and warm liquid trickled down my face, and I fought the urge to vomit where I laid. I'd never been in such horrific agony in my life, and I couldn't fight the heat filling my body as I slowly blinked my eyes. I tried to stay awake, I needed to. I was a fighter. I refused to give up.

I propped my hands under my body and pushed up from the ground, but it was useless. I didn't have the strength to support my body. A sharp kick landed in the middle of my back, and a shrill scream pierced my ears. Everything was moving slowly and then speeding up. I didn't have any concept of time. My face smacked against the hardwood, and the pain was too much. I couldn't fight it anymore.

Everything faded to black.

14

CROW

Ghoul called an impromptu meeting at the clubhouse to line everything out for when Heavy and the guys arrived. The more we talked about it, the hotter my blood boiled. If The Dogs hadn't tried to cut us out of the deal, none of this shit would be necessary. I was happy to see our brothers regardless of the reason, but I wished it was under better circumstances.

"What's the plan, Boss?" Wily mumbled over his cup of coffee, no doubt nursing his hangover.

Ghoul's light blue eyes trailed to me, and he tipped his head to the side. "What do you think, Crow? How should we handle them if and when they come knocking?"

"Not really sure, Ghoul. But if they are stupid enough to bring it to our doorstep, we'll be ready for whatever." I sipped my black coffee, thinking of the many ways we could torture them. Some people got their road names for noticeable physical traits, like Sledgehammer. He earned his name for the thing he called a dick. It more closely resembled a hammer, and he would nail anything that sat still long enough. The same could be said for Sac; his name left little to the imagination, and it was pretty apparent to people why we called him what we did. My name, on the other hand, was a little harder for people to figure out unless they were truly familiar with crows. They're adaptable birds that never forget a face, and often, the murder, a group of crows, will group together to hunt down a predator if it has killed one of their own. All of these things were true for me as well. I usually wasn't the first to draw blood, but if you fucked with us, I would find you by any means required and seek retribution. I might not remember everyone's name, but I would recognize their face as if it had been scorched into my mind.

"That's a damn sure thing," Circuit agreed, grabbing a broom, and sweeping dirt into a pile on the floor.

"How about we table this for now and discuss it further once Heavy arrives?" Wily prompted us, grabbing a hold of the discussion and bringing it to order since the subject was going nowhere fast. He was the best SAA I'd ever seen, and I was happy to call him brother. It was his job to keep us in line when it came to stuff like this, so he was usually the levelheaded one during the meetings.

We all consented and would have church on Wednesday after the DC chapter arrived. It gave us time to think about how to handle the situation...if there was one. I made a quick stop at the shop to check on everything.

Lonnie had just finished an oil change and was lowering the car off the rack as I walked through the doors. "How's everything, Lon?"

"Just getting ready to close down for the day. Did you need something?" He pulled his gloves off one at a time, lifting his hat and wiping the sweat off his brow on the sleeve of his jean uniform as he walked into the office to print out the customer's ticket.

"Nah, just checking on you guys while I had a few minutes. Need anything?" I followed him, taking the time to listen to the bell ding above the door—my favorite thing about the shop when I was a little boy. Dad used to get so pissed at me continuously opening and closing the door just to ring a bell. The strangest things that most did not give much thought to, ended up being the things your mind tied memories to.

"I think we're pretty good here," he mindlessly answered, his hand clicking away on the mouse. "No, scratch that. We're running low on plugs, brake shoes, wiper blades...Okay, we need to order some shit." He chuckled and raised his hands over his head as he shrugged.

"Write me up an item list and I'll order them Friday. Think we can make it until then?"

"Should be fine, if not, I'll have John run out and get what we need."

"Sounds good to me. Call me if you need anything in the meantime."

"Will do." He grabbed the brim of his ballcap and tipped it in my direction before giving his undivided attention to the customer. Lon had to be pushing eighty. He was one of the last workers Dad had hired before he passed away, and Lon wasn't young then. Per the government, he was only allowed to work so many hours, or he would lose his pension. Even when he wasn't working, he still came to the shop to drink coffee and bark orders at the younger employees. It wasn't a rare occurrence for me to slip his son, John, a wad of cash for him to sneak into his dad's house. When Lon would tell tales to us guys about him being one of the luckiest sons of a bitch since he always found extra cash laying around the house, I would grin and encourage him to continue with more stories.

On a general note, I wasn't an asshole, people only assumed I was. I lived by a code in and out of the club. I made it a point to ensure nothing illegal was intertwined with my business. It was one of the only aspects of my life I kept separate from the club. I refused to ruin Dad's name for my own profit. He might not have been there in all the conventional senses other fathers were, but he taught me how to be a fine businessman. I treated my employees well, and in turn, they kept the customers happy.

I drank too much and had almost lost count of the number of times a tattoo gun engraved ink into my skin, but that didn't mean I wasn't a good person...minus countless felonies. Who knew, had I moved out of Cleveland, my life might have taken an entirely different direction. Maybe I might have enrolled in the military or some shit. Truly, I had no clue. The possibilities were endless and pointless to consider because the blinding fact was, I hadn't moved out of Ohio and may never.

MY FAVORITE PART about riding wasn't hearing the power of the engine, although it was something I enjoyed. It was the serenity. When I was on my bike, things seemed right with the world. Time slowed just enough for me to break through my cloudy judgment and see things clearly. Although Ray and I hadn't spent much time together recently, it was almost as if we'd picked up where we left off except on better terms. I wasn't sure where we would end up, but I hoped it was together, and this time we would make it last. I would put in the work and not give up so easily. My mind was made up. As soon as I got home, I was going to lay it all out for her, and we could move forward. It was a ballsy move, but I wasn't known for being meek. I spoke my mind to everyone else, but with her, I held back, afraid of what she might think. Afraid I'd lose her again.

Slowing my speed and pulling into the driveway, the open front door caught my attention. I shook my head and smiled, figuring Ray had gone out to get some air and had forgotten to close it when she went inside. I didn't want to scare her, but I needed to ease her into the subject that it wasn't safe right now. I would protect her, without question, however, I couldn't do so if she did things like this.

The air was stale inside the house yet had a crispness to it. There was an undeniable lingering scent of blood that grew stronger with each step I took toward the living room. "Ray!" I yelled her name so loud and with such force, my body shook. Fuck. Where was she? I prayed to God that she was okay. Not like this. Shit. Fear throbbed through my veins, and I stumbled into the living room. A pool of blood was in the center of the room. It wasn't hers. It couldn't be hers. Tears stung my eyes, and I told myself to remain calm. I had to. The blood was streaked, and I could make out a small print. Her handprint. It was certainly too small to belong to a man.

"Ray. Please answer me!" I begged in a voice so weak I didn't even recognize it as my own, although my lips moved when it was said. Frantically, I searched all of the rooms in the house for her, but she wasn't here. "What have I done?" I sobbed into the empty house, calling her cell, praying she would answer and have a feasible explanation for all of this. I counted out the rings aloud, "One. Two. Come on, Ray. Three. Fucking answer. Four. Fuck!" I screamed when it went to voicemail. My knees kissed the floor, and I clasped my head in my hands after pulling Wily's name up on the screen.

"What's up?"

I cut him off, "Get here. Now." Ending the call, I let the phone slip from my hands and clatter to the floor in defeat. This was my fault. If I never stopped by her house, she would still be safe. The amount of horror I'd unintentionally brought into her life was unmeasurable. While I foolishly accepted her back into my life, the dread was pouring into hers by the gallons. I knew I would ruin her, but false hopes and expectations had me floating amongst a sea of blindness. I was too buoyant to rip the fucking blinders off to recognize that each time I touched her, all my transgressions seeped from my body into hers. She'd paid for my sin in blood.

Her voice tipped with a hint of playfulness echoed in my ears, "Are you bad like me?"

I had told her I was a fucking nightmare, knowing I would stain her innocence, but it was mostly a joke. I didn't actually believe the words as I spat them out. When I told her I was the fucking worst, the meaning of the statement hadn't sunken into my bones. Now, kneeling in a pool of what I could only assume to be her blood, I understood their true meaning.

I hated myself. My fingertips touched the bloody print of hers, and I whispered, "I'm sorry, Ray," as vicious uncontrollable sobs left my body. "I'm so sorry."

15

RAY

"Ray, grab the tacklebox, girl, and I don't mean the one in your face," Dad hollered from the truck right as I passed the garage. I grinned and flipped him off from where I stood. He was my best friend, other than my boyfriend, Logan. I loved going fishing with him because it meant time away from Mom. No matter how hard I tried, we didn't get along. I was always doing something wrong in her eyes, but I was trying my best, really I was.

I bent down to grab the tackle box and started getting sick to my stomach. "You okay? You're not looking so good." Dad's mouth was moving in sync with the words, but it wasn't his voice. It was one I heard before, though. I tried to move my hands, but they refused.

"Help me, Daddy," I cried as tears streaked my face, and I fell to my knees, unable to stand anymore.

Sadistic laughter pulled me into consciousness, and my eyelids flew open in response. I was far too weak to fight anyone off at the moment, but that didn't mean I wouldn't try anyway. I refused to give up.

"You can call me daddy if you like," a masked man

purred, running a long blade along my collarbone and grunted. "I'll give the Bastards one thing, they know how to pick 'em. This one is sweet." He clicked his tongue against the roof of his mouth and turned his head to the side. It was only then I realized he wasn't talking to me anymore, but the man standing across the room from us.

"Please. I have a savings account. I'll give you the pin, you can have all the money I have," I pleaded in a small voice as the room spun around me, knowing damn well they'd be even more pissed when they saw the little amount I was offering them.

"How sweet. She thinks she can right their wrongs. You can't so shut the fuck up and save your breath. You're going to need it for this next part." The guy across the room manically laughed. "Do it," he instructed the other man; he was the one in charge and calling the shots. He was the one I would have to convince to give me my freedom.

"Finally, if I wanted to listen to someone whine, I would have stayed at home." I made a mental note that he was married or at the very least had a significant other because of the ring on his finger. I'd seen enough crime shows to know little facts were important.

He jammed the tip of the blade through my skin, a tiny whimper passed through my lips, and I bit down on my bottom lip to muffle the noise. I didn't want to give them the satisfaction of knowing how bad it hurt. The rest of the knife ripped through my flesh with ease as if it were warm butter. It hadn't taken as much force as one would expect. The sound alone was enough to turn my stomach; it was like a rare steak being ripped apart against the grain. A tormented scream flowed up my throat and surrounded all of my senses. I couldn't concentrate on anything else other than the pain, so I focused on it to even my breathing out as I gritted my teeth.

"I think she likes it." He sounded amused, enjoying his torture of me.

I spat on his shoe; I couldn't help it. I'd never been a pushover, and I was too stupid to be one now.

"You bitch!" he growled, backhanding my cheek. My body flew sideways, my cheekbone smacking against the floor, and instantly, an unrelenting throbbing sting pounded in distress. I didn't move or speak; I didn't have the power within me this time. The coolness of the stone floor was soothing and welcoming. My eyes fluttered as I fought the fall into nothingness, but it took me prisoner yet again.

16

CROW

Ghoul and Wily hooked their biceps under my arms and lifted me to my feet. "We're going to get her, brother. Sit tight and we'll handle it," Ghoul assured me and wrapped his arm around my waist, letting me go when I waved my hands in the air.

"No!" A sharp tone rattled up my windpipe as I clutched the note Diablo found taped to my door. I'd passed right by it because I was in too much of a hurry to get to Ray. It was from The Dogs and they had the audacity to sign it:

Bastards,
  You took our money and torched our fucking warehouse, so we took this sweet ass. She's just the first of many. Bodies will continue to disappear until we get our money. Bring what we're owed plus 50K to the rendezvous point tonight at 1800 hours, and we'll call it square.
  P.S. I would hurry. Monster isn't known for his patience in matters such as this. You'll be lucky if this

dumb bitch lives to see daylight again. Who knows, she might if she's a good little girl.

With love,

Dogs of Chaos

"I'm going to fucking kill every last one of those fuckers!" I swore, getting to my feet, and Wily stood between the door and me.

"Crow, we have to form a plan," he slowly articulated, walking toward me, his palms swatting at the air as he took another step closer, trying to calm me down.

"Alright, what's the fucking plan?" I insisted, punching a nearby support beam of the house, my knuckles crunched against the wood, and blood spattered the adjacent wall.

"Call the rest of the guys," Ghoul instructed Diablo and Wily, "Tell them we're on our way and to be at the clubhouse. Mandatory. No excuses."

"You got it, boss," Diablo quickly replied, pressing his fingers to the keypad of his burner phone.

"Flashman, what kind of explosives do you have at your place?" Wily eyed him, getting right to the point as soon as he called the meeting to order.

"I have enough shit to light their asses up like it's the Fourth of July." His lips spread into a wide grin, and he shoved a cigar between them.

"Sac and I will get all the counterfeit bills, and we're going to stuff them into one of the hot vehicles Diablo picked up a few weeks ago. A 2020 'Vette should cover fifty thou and then some, right?"

Diablo nodded his head.

"Right. So, we stuff the bags of cash in the backseat, and you line the bottom of that fucker with as much shit as your little heart desires, Flash."

"Fucking, right." Ghoul nodded in agreement, glancing over to me. "We don't kill a damn one of them until we tail them back to Crow's nurse."

"I want that part. I'm going to make them regret the day they ever fucked with the Royal Bastards," I spoke for the first time since we reached the clubhouse.

"'Course, brother. Wouldn't have it any other way. Spider, you and Sleeper stay back in case we need back up. Oh, and get a hold of Heavy, fill him in on the details." Ghoul made sure everyone had an assignment, not giving anyone time to get a word in edgewise. "Sledge, you're with Diablo and Flash." He pointed his finger toward their end of the table. "Wily, you're with Crow and me." Unmistakable rage bounded from his words, and he pounded his fists against the table.

"All in agreement?" Wily sounded off, always remembering to keep things official.

"Aye," we all yelled in unison.

17

CROW

Everything had gone smoothly so far, and the minutes ticked by agonizingly slow. I couldn't wait to get to Ray, but as soon as she was safe, I was making The Dogs pay. Even if it wouldn't have been my fault that Ray was in the middle of our MC war, I would still get revenge. The pressing fact was that it was my fault, and I cared about her, so it was personal. I usually tried not to involve my feelings when it came to club shit, it made you a liability. A person's head didn't think clearly when emotions were thick and fogged their judgment. I tried to remind myself of all these things as Ghoul, Wily, and I sat quietly, not so patiently waiting for The Dogs to take us back to Ray.

"C'mon, fleabags. Take the money and get us back to the nurse," Ghoul mumbled in a hushed tone, his impatience spreading as thin as mine. "That's it," he coaxed them as a couple of them climbed in the Corvette, no doubt to count the money.

A guy flashed a light to the driver in the unmarked van, and the side door slid open. There she was. We were too far away to make out how much they made her suffer because of us. A guy shoved the barrel of a rifle in the middle of her back and forced her out of the van, urging her to her knees.

A deep, primal growl ripped out of my mouth, and Ghoul's arm fingertips dug into my upper arm while he held me in place. "Just a few more minutes, brother. Wait for it."

As soon as the gun was off Ray, Diablo was the first to move, creating a distraction so we could move in for the kill. Diablo raised his gun, and one of his slugs landed in the man's body who had the rifle. We were quick on our feet and came into the clearing before anyone else could fire another round. I wanted to grab Ray and never let her go, but now more than ever, my brothers needed me.

I ran to her side. "I have you, Ray. It's all going to be okay," I assured her, clutching her to my chest and drew my judge, aiming toward the driver and squeezing the trigger. Momentarily, my ears rang from the loudness of the shot, and I could feel Ray's mouth moving against my body, but had no clue what she was trying to tell me. She lifted on her feet high enough to push her body into mine, and she went limp.

"Fuck," I screamed, rolling over and hot tears burned my eyes. "Why did you do that you stupid girl? Ray!" I yelled, and my throat instantly suffered from the force. Bullets were zooming and blood was flying all around us, but I couldn't move.

"Because," her eyes finally moved, and her chest rose, "Someone has to save your ass." A corner of her mouth pulled into a half-smirk, and I gathered her hands, pushing them against her stomach where the blood was coming from.

"I fucking love you, Ray. Always have," I quickly declared, not certain I'd ever get another chance. I lifted her from the ground and laid her in the back of the van. It wasn't an ideal place, but she should be safe in there.

"I know you do." She weakly laughed, and her eyes widened in fear as she sucked in a frightened breath. "Crow. Ghoul," was all she managed to say, but it was all I needed. I turned on my feet as fast as lighting, running, and swiftly grabbed the judge off the ground, pointing it as soon as it was in my clutches. It took a second to find Ghoul, his temple was at the end of a barrel, and I didn't hesitate. Applying pressure with my index finger, another bullet soared through the air, and the guy's lifeless body dropped to the ground.

The remaining two cowards took off in the Corvette, but it didn't matter, Flash would take care of them. It was just a matter of time. He let them get a good hundred feet down the clearing and then fire lifted the car off the ground before it plummeted back down to the earth and continued to burn.

"Damn. He wasn't kidding." I whistled and accessed the situation. All my brothers were accounted for, which meant getting Ray to the hospital was the priority right now.

18

RAY

"Going to a party isn't taking it easy, Ray," Logan said gritting his teeth and running his hand through his hair, trying to remain calm, but clearly not doing a very good job. "Really, we can skip this one. Ghoul will understand."

"Maybe, but we really need to be around other people before we kill each other." I smiled, knowing it wasn't him I was worried about. He was smothering me, watching my every movement, but he meant well. I couldn't hate him for caring too much, however, it was foreign to me to have someone else care for me. Yet, it seemed the moment I arrived in Ohio, it was what everyone else was doing. Thinking back, even Dad was doing that as he laid in the hospital bed and helped me dream up my future. It didn't matter how strong a person believed they are, they all needed help from someone else. Even when they were too stubborn to recognize it.

EPILOGUE

CROW

Heavy and the guys stuck around until Ray was in the clear and then planned a shindig. I helped Ray, and just like the first time she came through the doors of the clubhouse, Ghoul immediately untangled himself from Red to talk to us.

"Nurse, you're looking good. Let me introduce you to some brothers from our other chapters." My eyes narrowed in his direction, but we all knew Ray had not only saved my life, but she also saved Ghoul's, too. We both had her to thank for us being alive.

"Heavy, this is...wait, what are you all talking about?" Ghoul stopped with the introductions, and we all listened to them.

"Sledge, heard you got your name from that thrill hammer between your legs. Ya know, we're always looking for new stars in the biz, right? Drop that beaut out and let's measure them side by side," Heavy said before tipping the shot back and clapping Sledge on the back.

The fucker was really gonna do it. Sledge pinched his zipper and made it halfway down before Ghoul spoke up, shaking his head, "I've fucking seen it all. You two really are going to have a dick measuring contest. Shit." He rubbed his eyes and squeezed the bridge of his nose. "How about we bust out some liquor instead and drink in honor of my nurse. She saved not only this stubborn fucker's life," his left hand landed in the middle of my chest, "But my ass, too."

Ray's cheeks blushed, and she cleared her throat. "Ghoul, I didn't save your ass, Crow did."

"I might have been the one to fire the shot, but had you not told me..." My words stopped as quickly as they began, the whole subject was hard for me to talk about.

"Aye. Let's not talk about depressing shit, this is a celebration, bitches." Sac elbowed his way to the bar, and all of our heads turned to him.

"Fuck. Somebody take him outside and blaze one. None of us are prepared to see Sac without any weed in his system," I warned, picking up on his unbridled hyperness.

"Not until we do a shot, then I'll get him higher than Lady Liberty herself," Diablo piped up, "If that's okay with you, boss?"

"Fine by me. Fine by me," he repeated, lifting his shot glass into the air. "To my little sister and nurse, Ray. This one is just for us." He slid a shot to her and smiled. "The doctor is still seeing patients, thanks to you." They flipped back the whiskey, and Ghoul pushed their glasses across the bar to Diablo for a refill. "This one is for my brothers."

We all pushed our way through to grab our shot, knowing what was coming. "Forever Bastard, Bastard Forever," we all proudly chanted. Some of the brothers showed their appreciation by shaking her hand while others gave her a nod of approval, but all of them made it a point to do something as they passed us. A large number of them clapped me on the back after hearing I was the one who took out the coward holding Ghoul at gunpoint, and I politely thanked them. However, if it hadn't been for Ray, neither of us would have made it to see the next day.

I never guessed when she walked into my life this is where we would end up, especially given the tragic beginning. All stories had to start somewhere I guessed, but when you were a Bastard like me, one couldn't predict how it would end. Hell, I still didn't know, but we were taking life one day at a time.

ACKNOWLEDGMENTS

THANK YOU TO EVERYONE WHO HAS MADE THIS PUBLICATION POSSIBLE.

To the readers, bloggers, fellow authors, and everyone in the book community: Thank you for letting us be a part of our ever-changing world. It's hard to accept this is our life. They never thought they would essentially be coworkers; afraid the world may implode if it happened. Thankfully, the only things being destroyed are on the pages of a book.

Harmony: Thank you so much for just being you. You may be small, but the amount of love your capable of giving us is boundless. You will eventually outgrow our arms, but never our hearts. We love you, Tinkerbell!

Eli Abbott: I'm adding this while you're asleep, because you can't change it if you know it's here...until it's too late that is. We've been through more than I care to think about over the past couple of months. Most of which were uncontrollable. I love you husband and literally couldn't do any of this without you. Thank you for being a friend when I need it and the love of my life. I love you, husband.

Maria Vickers: Thank you for busting your ass to get this finished. You are so freaking amazing and we're so thankful for you!

To my street team, Crazed Lunatics: Thank you for every share, like, word of encouragement, and for just being you. Y'all are my people and my tribe. #AreYouALunatic #CrazyAsChelle #AcaciaMalone #Eli Abbott

Letha Gene: We love you! Thank you for letting the tiny tornado stay a few nights with you all. Keep writing and fighting each day to overcome anything the world throws your way. You're strong willed and that determination can take you just about anywhere you want it to.

Becky Hensley: Thank you so much for reading this and just plain being you. Happy late birthday, again.

3: I don't even know where to begin or to end. I love you and someday all the promised tackle hugs between us will happen. I feel sorry for the people standing by to witness it, though. -snort laugh Imagine the shock of two grown women knocking each other down with a hug.

Sean Moriarty & Izzy Sweet: We're so lucky to call you all family. We're always here for you all, just call us...or drive here. Doesn't matter to us. Love you, guys.

To the participating authors of The Royal Bastards MC: Thank you for welcoming us into the family and being there when we needed someone. You all are phenomenal writers and we're going to rock this!

ABOUT THE AUTHOR

Thank you for reading! Chelle and Eli is a dynamic husband and wife duo native to West Virginia. Their biggest inspiration and blessing will always be their daughter.

More books by Chelle C. Craze & Eli Abbott are coming soon. Don't worry!
Chelle also writes paranormal under her pen name Acacia Malone.

Visit her website, www.ChelleCCraze.com, or find them on social media.

Facebook:
https://www.facebook.com/AuthorChelleCCraze
https://www.facebook.com/AuthorEliAbbott

Facebook for Paranormal and Paranormal Romance:
https://www.facebook.com/AuthorAcaciaMalone
Goodreads: https://www.goodreads.com/author/show/7111512.Chelle_C_Craze

Wattpad:
https://www.wattpad.com/user/CrazyAsChelle

- bookbub.com/profile/chelle-ccraze
- amazon.com/author/chelleccraze
- facebook.com/AuthorChelleCCraze
- twitter.com/ChelleCCraze
- instagram.com/chelleccraze

OTHER BOOKS BY CHELLE C. CRAZE:

Just Breathe Book One of The Blue Series

Waiting to Breathe Book Two of The Blue Series

Chaos Book One of The Blackwell Bayou Series

Proof Book Two of The Blackwell Bayou Series

Kamikaze Heart Book One of Cupid's Aim & Book 2.5 of The Blackwell Bayou Series

Dahlia Book Five of The ScentSations Empire

Plush Book One of the Life and Death Saga by Acacia Malone

Scars of My Brother CRMC Boon One by Chelle C. Craze & Eli Abbott

Hard Rime A Forever Safe Christmas Book 3 & Dogs of Chaos MC Book One

Printed in Great Britain
by Amazon